Keep your head down. even think about technology if one of those ghostly, grey cars is sliding silently down the road. They'll see the thoughts inside you, if you let them.

Sam's a technopath, able to control electronic signals and manipulate technology with his mind. And so, ever since childhood, his life has been a carefully constructed web of lies, meant to keep his Talent hidden, his powers a secret. But the Institute wants those unusual powers, and will do anything to get a hold of him and turn him into one of their mindless slaves.

Sam slips up once. Just once, but that's enough. Now the Institute is after him in full force. Soldiers, telekinetics, and mind readers, all gunning just for him.

Newly qualified soldier, Serena, doesn't even know she's chasing a person, all she knows is that she has to find whatever the Institute is after before they do. But tracking an unknown entity through an unfamiliar city, with inaccurate intelligence, unexpected storms, and Gav Belias, people's hero of the Watch, on the prowl, will she even survive? Will she get to Sam before the Institute does? His special skills could provide the rebellion with an incredible advantage, but not if they can't get out of the city, and over the huge wall that stands between them and freedom.

# I Am the Storm

## The Psionics, Book One

*Tash McAdam*

A NineStar Press Publication

Published by NineStar Press
P.O. Box 91792,
Albuquerque, New Mexico, 87199 USA.
www.ninestarpress.com

# I Am the Storm

Printed in the USA
First Edition
December, 2018

Print ISBN: 978-1-949909-72-2

Also available in eBook, ISBN: 978-1-949909-70-8

Warning: This book contains scenes of violence.

For Marie {even though}

# Part One

# Sam

I DIDN'T ASK to be Talented, but I am, and because of that, I endanger everyone around me. Every day. The government wants people like me under their control, or dead. So we hide the best we can out here in the shadowy and factory district. It's hot, same as always, even in the shade. Out here isn't much to look at—especially compared to the inner city, which sparkles like diamonds. Around me, buildings in grays and browns loom into the blue sky, blocking the vicious sun and removing the need for the transparent aluminum shields guarding the open spaces from the UV. Those are for the rich.

This area is always in the darkness. We're part of the City, but only just. Pressed up against the inside of the Wall, this end of town really isn't much better than the slums. Nah, shit, I take it back. At least I've always had a roof over my head and food in my belly, even if it tastes pretty bland. My mom made sure of that.

People in the slums aren't as lucky. Mom moved us out to the poor end of town because of me—it's obvious, even if she lies whenever it comes up. She had a good job back before I was born, as a teacher in one of the elite elementary schools, and she loved it. I hear in her voice how much her heart aches when she tells stories about her old students. Now, she pulls levers fifteen hours a day in a plant and can't stand up straight anymore. It's my fault.

I'm snapped out of my musing by a warning shout and barely avoid a speeding mini elec-car, piled high with boxes and strips of metal. A second later, I'd have been another smear marring the tarmaxx. No point in putting solar panels here, after all, so the road is far from shiny and clean. I curse at the driver's back.

Shoving my hands into my pockets, I chew my lip and dawdle down the road. I'm not in a hurry. Medical exams are one of my least favorite pastimes, but if I want to stay in school, and damn straight that's what I want, I have to go. Being weighed, prodded, and poked isn't nearly as fun as going home and relaxing with a hacked satellite feed, but we do what we must, right? Since I have these checkups twice yearly, along with every other Citizen in our glorious metropolis, I know how late I can be—without getting penalized—to the second. Although, I don't have any idea what the time actually is since I don't even have my comm unit with me. For once, I don't have any tech in my pockets, and it makes me feel naked and exposed.

But it's the only way I can keep from blowing my cover.

I'm a lucky sod, for sure. As a technopath—able to control technology with my mind—I have a unique power, and I'm not noticeable the way telekinetics are. They throw stuff around with their Talent. Obvious stuff right there. Me? Hell, if I get really angry, I can cause a blackout, but it's doubtful anyone would trace it back to me. Living in an area without electricity helps, though. Thanks, Ma.

Giving up the creature comforts for your only son is a noble thing to do, and it's kept me under the radar for years. Off the radar and above ground, instead of locked up in a facility designed to destroy any aspect of me deemed not "useful." So, you know, my memories, my personality, and sense of self, for a start. If the Institute had their way and nabbed me as one of their brainwashed weapons, I'd lose everything making me myself.

I should get a bit of a move on, though. If you're not there when they call your name a third time, you get bounced off the list and marked as "uncooperative," which isn't a good thing. They watch the uncooperative, in case we're considering a life of rebellion and insurrection. And I'm exactly the kind of person they'd love to catch. Besides being Talented, I do my fair share of cybercrime. They'd only have to watch me for a few days before I ended up with a hood over my head and a gun in my spine. I might not be tall, strong, or rich, but I'm definitely dangerous.

I pick up the pace a little and, rushing around the next corner, thud right into the broad chest of a watchman. I stumble and lose my balance, and then I'm knocked off my feet by a powerful and unnecessary uppercut to the jaw. I cry out in pain, rebounding off the wall and crumpling in a heap.

Blinking back stinging tears of shock, I clap my palm to my throbbing face. The brute looks down at me, pathetic Sam, crouched on the ground, wearing worn-out clothes. He spits on me, daring me to retaliate so he can arrest me and throw me in the clink. Power tripping. The Watch—military police—are government thugs, but many of them aren't bad people. Just people with a sucky job.

This one appears to be your standard petty thug in a uniform.

I cringe away enough to make him think I'm respectful, but he still raises his boot, so I drop my eyes, every inch the persecuted worker. It's enough. He decides not to go through with the kick and heads off instead, whistling tunelessly. I stay down until he's around the next bend. Then I close my eyes and suck a thread of technopathic

Talent out of the ever-comforting ball of power waiting inside me, longing to be used. The invisible strength has been a part of me for longer than I can remember, and it fills me with confidence. I can operate any piece of electronic machinery in the world without even touching it.

Twisting my fingers to the side, I unleash the power, sending it after him, honing in on his gadgets. The movement isn't usually necessary—I could do this with my mind alone, on any other day—but the pain spiking through my jawbone is distracting, and physical motion gives me an extra layer of control.

When the power reaches him, I use it to blow out every single one of the circuits on his equipment. It's going to look as though he's been in a huge electricity surge but somehow escaped personal damage. I grin, despite my aching jaw. I wish I could melt the soles of his shoes, too, but that's outside my abilities. I can only manipulate electricity, not create it. Unless there's a handy lightning strike in the next few minutes for me to redirect, I'm stuck with the piddly amperage of his equipment.

Next time Mr. Watchman checks his equipment, he's going to be in trouble, which makes me feel better. Not much, but a smidge. However, if I'm late to the clinic, I'll have more than a bruise to worry about, so I stand and jog the rest of the way, wincing as it jars my rapidly swelling left cheek and jaw.

I know I look out of place as soon as I enter the clean white room, sweaty and bruised with pale hair sticking to my forehead in annoying streaks. And I even wore my best outfit—only two visible patches! Disapproving eyes belonging to the wealthy and well-dressed scan me, their faces twisting into disdainful expressions.

Not many factory kids are Citizens, with the privilege of a decent education and medical care. There are no such tests for my "peers." I'm here because I was born in the City and had enough early education to take the tests and get into school. My friends aren't here, because they weren't, and didn't. It's hard to get a decent start in life when your parents work all the time and can't afford real day care. Worse—if you're born outside the Wall, they don't want you here, so the schooling test is weighted against you.

The slum kids hardly ever have a chance of attending school. It's all so stupid; there are kids working the line who are way smarter than me but never really learned to read. Of course, they failed the tests we had to take when we were eleven. If you can't understand the question, how are you supposed to answer it? The whole system sucks.

My mom made sure I got a good start to my education, though, courtesy of her own knowledge, so I passed the tests. I got into real school. Hence my tightrope-walking act between privilege and poverty. A working-class kid with a middle-class right to basic amenities. Which means following rules other factory kids don't have to follow. Taking these medical tests, for example.

These clinics are the most dangerous places I ever have to go because they belong to the government and are the heart of enemy territory; one slipup and I'm worse than dead. I take a slow breath, forcing myself to push my power into dormancy and ignore it.

I slide up to the desk. "Sam Dovzhenko." My voice rings loud and out of place in the silence that always fills waiting rooms, as though everyone is afraid to breathe.

The receptionist looks down his bladed nose at me and sniffs. It's an eloquent sniff, one saying "What are you doing here?" but he checks his holoscreen anyway. I wait, bored. I could type faster when I was ten and have to suppress the urge to make his computer system change his input. Always fun, messing with the snobs.

He finally finds my information and hands me a plastic card so thin it's almost invisible. As soon as I take it from his clammy hand, it lights up, blue lines tracing a map of the clinic and a dot showing my position. Another glowing bead indicates where I should go, and the receptionist raises his eyebrow at me as though he expects me to need help reading a map.

*Don't wipe his hard drive, don't wipe his hard drive.* I repeat to myself as I head through the large metal door leading to the main body of the clinic. My power can get away from me when I'm irritated or angry, not ideal in a place like this. Or anywhere, really, even at school. It's a huge pain in the butt to know I could relax and put my feet up while my datapad churns out exactly what I want in the most efficient way possible when I'm handed a new project. But definitely better than what would happen to me if people found out what I'm capable of.

The ability to "talk" to computers is the most incredible gift I could ask for. But my gift could also get me abducted, experimented on—oh—and wiped of all personality. So letting my control slip in a lab belonging to the very government that wants to experiment on me is a bad idea.

Willing myself to be calm, I traipse along the gleaming corridor, a superpowered vagabond in a laboratory. I didn't understand I was different for a long time. I guess when I was really small I assumed everyone could absorb and interpret wireless signals and affect electrical currents. I can control their throughput, and it allows me to telepathically interact with any technology.

My mom says I was around three months old when I first turned the lights in my room on with my mind. I probably did it because I hated the dark. I still hate it.

Mom packed up, left my dad, and hightailed it out of there in the middle of the night. Sounds harsh, but my dad works for the government, and as such, is likely to be scanned psionically. Telepathically. They do it to everyone who works for them—scan their brains to find out what they know.

If he had any inkling what I could do, he'd put me in danger, whether he wanted to or not. It doesn't matter if you want to give somebody up to the bad guys when they just reach into your head and rummage around. I didn't see him again until I was six or so—old enough to understand how I was different and how to control it.

We don't have much to talk about these days, but he's a good guy. Takes me to ball games sometimes and bitches because my mom won't take anything from him—no money or help.

Poverty is a great excuse to avoid linking up our whole house though—and I'd be bound to eventually mess up in front of someone if I lived in a "smart" house. Especially when I was younger and had less control. I'd end up shutting the blinds with my mind when I was half asleep or something, then boom. Game over. And as an extra piece of protection, not living in a nice area means the mind readers are less likely to catch me.

The Institute—government-sponsored jerks who get their rocks off abducting baby telepaths and screwing with their brains—mostly stick to the nicer sections when they're after spies. They also spend a lot of time in the slums, looking for potential slaves they might have missed at birth. But I'm smack bang in the middle, and why would anyone with powers be here?

A blast of cold air makes me jump. A doctor banging out of a freeze-room, probably. I move out of her way in a hurry and then take a right, following the map. I'm a little jittery with nerves, but hopefully anyone who sees me thinks it's natural for a poor kid in a rich place. A lot of the tests they run really hurt, which could explain my twitchiness. Great.

I get to my destination and wrinkle my nose as I see the light above the shiny door is red. There's an uncomfortable-looking bench to wait on, but I choose to lean my bony shoulder against the wall, instead. I'm never comfortable relaxing in places like this. Too clean. It makes me feel as though I'm going to get in trouble.

People bustle past, lab coats flapping and clipboards clacking, and I tune in carefully to the signals scooting around the place. Someone's watching a TV show about space, computers are sending files back and forth, and there's a pretty racy conversation going on between the guy at the front desk and someone called "LeatherCowboy21." Passively watching signals isn't very risky. It also lets me keep an eye on what's going on—if any Institute messages are coming in or going out. And it gives me something to do.

Suddenly, though, a particularly shocking image from Cowboy to the receptionist makes me flinch, and my Talent skids out of me, shooting toward the nearest electrical circuit. Before I can stop it, it hits the ceiling lights, and they flicker. *Shit, shit.* I look up and down the corridor from under my fringe, attempting to be unobtrusive. My heart racing, I carefully slide out of the signals I've been piggybacking on, compressing my power as far as it goes. I feel sick, as though I've been punched in the stomach. How could I be such an idiot, here, of all places? I'm right under their noses, and I thought I could fiddle around without getting caught? I actually thought it was safe?

Nobody comes for me, though, and my heart rate slowly returns to normal.

The door light clicks to green and a mellow-voiced robot woman calls out, "Sam Dovzhenko. Sam Dovzhenko to room sixteen, please." Soaked in fear sweat, terror clawing at my ribcage, I stretch my neck, take a deep breath, and prepare for the indignities to come.

The door slides back as soon as I touch it, almost gliding out of my way. Inside, the room is shiny and smallish, with a padded bed and various buzzing machines, all of which are filling the air with information. The doctor sits at a large desk, a huge computer array in front of him.

Forgetting my fear for a split second, I automatically assess the capabilities of the machine. Looks like a stallion, works like a pony, as my mom would say. Usually about men, though. Gross.

The doctor looks at me over his compu-spec and doesn't smile. It's a deliberate non-movement of the facial muscles, as though he's trying not to grimace at my appearance, so, palms slick, I give him my best grin. The one saying "I'm adorable; you can trust me, yes sir! Why, I'm just a sweet, sweet child trapped in bad circumstances." I practice it in the mirror. I'm not a handsome guy, but I can pull off cute, and this is the face I use at school when people are picking on me for bringing lunch in a box instead of paying for canteen food. Look harmless enough and some people will start to feel guilty for treating you like dog dirt. Not everyone, of course, but any advantage you can get is worth taking, in my opinion. Especially if you screwed up monumentally and are possibly about to get arrested.

He seems to buy it, softening slightly and gesturing me to the chair in front of the desk, then turning his attention from me, his eyes glazing over for a moment. I assume he's looking at information on the miniscreen over his left eye, and wait.

A moment later, he comes back to me. "Sam Dovzhenko, fourteen-point-seven years old, classified as a Citizen after outstanding test scores." It's a musing tone, not requiring an answer, and I wait expectantly for him to continue. "Last checkup showed slight signs of malnutrition. You were provided with a free scrip for vitamins. I see you've been collecting them. Good boy. Anything you want to raise with me?"

I manage not to clench my jaw at his patronizing tone. I brought it on myself with the baby face, I think wryly. Sigh. I shake my head.

The doctor gets to his feet, having to heave himself up with the arms of his chair. Overweight. I wonder what his checkup is going to say about his weight. I bet he has a system with one of the other doctors in the clinic allowing him to get through the tests even when he shouldn't. Hypocrite. Tell me I'm malnourished when you clearly eat enough to feed an entire family.

Knowing what's coming, I follow his example and stand up. He motions me over to the padded bed, and I sit on the edge so he can check my eyes, ears, throat, nervous system, and heartbeat. Then comes the sucky stuff. Cancer suppressants are the absolute worst part of the medicals for me, but I can't get out of them. I've tried. I grit my teeth as he preps the hollow needle and sucks the suspended nanobots—miniature robots that will zoom through my blood, finding any mutated cells and destroying them—into the plunger. The silvery fluid shoots up and fills the plastic part of the syringe, where it swirls ominously. The last time I did this, a year ago, I passed right out when the doctor punched the little buggers into my jugular. But this time I'm determined not to. Or...maybe I will.

He presses his fingers against my neck, looking for the throbbing artery. My pulse is going a mile a minute already, anticipating the stabbing pain followed by the awful sensation of liquid forced into my body.

I pull the digital representation of the space show I noticed earlier up onto the ceiling to distract me. I shouldn't, but I know this will hurt so badly I can barely force myself to stay on the bed. I need something else to look at.

On the screen, some cowboy-looking guy is climbing from a spaceship ramp onto a dusty planet. The picture loses a lot in binary format. I wish I could get the detail, but it's impossible; my power is green, so if I use it to see something, then what I watch is in green, which means the picture kind of sucks. I don't know what it's like for other Readers—people who use telepathy as an extra sense, getting information from their surroundings—but for me, this is as good as it gets.

The needle touches my skin lightly and then jabs in. It's pretty much as bad as I expected, but I don't actually pass out this time. Macho.

I do, however, squeeze my eyes shut and clamp down on my power, which fizzes in indignation at the control and its need to break free. It busts free when I'm upset or hurt, and if I don't keep a tight grip on it, I could blow every circuit in the building. But I don't usually lose control these days. I've been practicing. Breathing deeply through my nose helps, and I count as I force myself to relax. The needle finally pulls out, dragging against the soft skin of my throat, and I can't repress a little whimper of pain. Google, I hate this.

The doctor gives me one of those looks meaning "Are you a man, or a mouse?" that always irritates me. The annoyance distracts me from the throbbing sensation, and he presses a small square of cloth against the wound before I notice. Then he grabs the suture gun with the other.

The sutures thud into my skin while he holds my head in place. They don't hurt quite as badly as the injection, but I'm still having tiny staples stabbed into me, crisscrossing over the new hole in my artery. Two minutes later I'm patched up and ready for the chest X-rays and measuring portion of the checkup.

It's boring and uneventful, and I can never figure out why they want to do it in this order, instead of letting the worst part come at the end. All I want to do is curl up in a ball and maybe have a little cry, but instead, I have to stay in front of them, obeying their stupid requests, running a pathetically slow mile on a treadmill, half naked. The doctor looks at my skinny chest, ribs visible, noticeable dent in the center, and shakes his head. I'm clearly not as muscular as he would prefer.

You can talk, chubby.

I'm panting and sweaty by the time he allows me to sit again and busies himself at the pretty-on-the-outside computer. I'm expected to wait, like a good boy, for my results to be popped onto my thumb chip. But I'm anxious to get out of here. The myriad of hoops I've jumped through have left me exhausted, and keeping my power under wraps is getting harder and harder. It wants to burst out of me and punish the people who are hurting me. To distract myself so I don't lose control, I push against the hard point in my thumb where I feel the lump of technology I, and every Citizen, have to carry everywhere.

I love my thumb chip, but mostly because it provides a fantastic focal interface for me. My power means I can use any computer in existence, regardless of security and complexity, but I need a place to start. And the government conveniently put one in place for me—right in my thumb.

Minicomputer in the hands of the computer guy. Idiots. I don't think they know people like me exist, but here I am. And there's probably more out there. I did the math, once. Around ten percent of the population are telepaths, according to the Institute's files; I had a look-see a few years ago, just to keep ahead of the game. Had to follow a crew around and stay out of sight so I could jump onto their network, but it was worth it. It's unlikely I'd be the only technopath, even if it is clearly rarer.

The doctor clears his throat, shaking me from my thoughts, and I start. He waggles a device at me, and I obediently place my right thumb on the datapad, blinking innocently. I'm capable of changing whatever data I want on the chip in my thumb. These chips are how we use money, and also how the government keeps track of us, but I rig mine so it reports I'm at home, like a good boy, no matter what I'm actually doing. Nothing too nefarious, but sometimes knowing I'm off grid is a good feeling. Freeing.

Right now I'd give anything to be feeling free, but there's a sick sensation in my stomach that I don't think can be tied to the injection. Something is off. The way the doctor's looking at me sets my teeth on edge.

The transparent screen lights up in a series of green gridlines, zooming smaller as they get to my digit, indicating the transfer of data, and I parse it carefully as it inputs. I think it's worth the risk, to know what they're saying. If they've marked me. But it's nothing surprising; a standard report of my physical non-prowess.

When it's done, and the lights go off with a depressed-sounding beep, I glance at the doctor for permission and he nods. I remove my hand and fold it carefully back into my lap. He doesn't say anything else, and I stand, planning on removing myself from the unpleasant room—and pressing danger—as soon as possible.

But he lifts his hand in a "hold it" motion. I freeze, halfway out of my chair, and then lower myself back into the seat, wondering what he wants. My foot jitters nervously, and I grit my teeth as I force myself to become still.

"We have a few more tests to run today, unfortunately. If you'll wait here, I'll get the nurse to come and take care of it. Nothing to worry about."

Liar. There's always something to worry about. Right now more than ever. I messed up. I know it. The air freezes in my lungs, and my mind starts whirring until I barely stop myself from flinging my body out of the chair and making a break for it. But running would be a dead giveaway, and I don't know for sure I'm busted. I just really, really think I am. If I'm not, then running for it is a terrible idea. The lump in my throat makes breathing difficult, and my hand slips on the arm of the chair, where I've apparently been tightly clutching the plastic. My muscles ache as they move.

The doctor bustles out of the room, a small screen clutched in one hairy paw, and I flick my eyes from side to side. Should I bail now? A loud noise behind me makes me jump, skidding the chair sideways in fear, a horrible screech filling the air as the legs drag across the smooth floor. Jerking around, I see it's only a nurse, looking at me in surprise. The sound was obviously the small, wheeled table she's pushing in front of her. She must have banged the door with it to tell it to open.

I'm terrified, cold sweat making my palms and neck clammy. I just want to get out of here. But the nurse smiles at me kindly, her warm brown eyes comforting. "Did I make you jump? I'm sorry, dear. Here, hop up on the bed for me, and we'll get you started. We need a couple of blood samples to see how your body is dealing with the cancer suppressant."

Oh. Okay. More needles, but no danger. Okay. My heartbeat slows its madcap gallop, and I nod, stumbling over my own big feet as I get up and head for the bed again to take a seat. It'll be okay. The air in the room is thick, and I'm too hot, but my fingers and toes are freezing.

"Lie down, in case you take a funny turn." Arm muscles bulging, she maneuvers the table across to the end of the bed and fiddles with a needle. Lovely. Not knowing what else to do, I obey and spin around, putting my feet up, uncomfortably aware of how dirty I am compared to the white material covering the gurney. She fusses for a few more moments and then picks up my arm, which she probes with her thumb, gloved hands confident. She flicks the liquid-filled syringe, and I look away, not wanting to watch my blood swirl up into the syringe.

The full syringe.

The sharp prick of the needle hits me at the exact same moment as the realization that she can't possibly be about to take my blood with an already full syringe. The cry bubbles up out of me, and I try to snatch my arm away, but the liquid is already pumping into my bloodstream, a dragon roaring through my veins. It's a freight train, unstoppable as it runs me over. My yell emerges stillborn, a soft squeak all that escapes my mouth, and blackness wraps cold arms around me, sucking me away from the world.

The lights go off as I disappear.

# Serena

I BITE THE inside of my cheek so hard the thick, metallic taste of blood coats my tongue. Normally I'd be resisting the urge to bare my teeth for the gory effect, but not now. Don't cry, for freedom's sake, don't cry. My eyes sting, making it difficult to keep my gaze steely and focused, as befits the soldier I just failed at becoming. The smell of cordite and burning is thick in the air, and I tell myself it's the swirling gray smoke causing the tears prickling at the corners of my eyes.

The wash of orange illuminating the faux alleyways casts an unnatural pallor over the dark walls, adding to the forbidding atmosphere. The blinking red light flashing above the passage I limped from denotes my failure and forms an angry halo behind the stocky man towering over me.

Kion Arbalast—one of my own personal heroes—scrunches his heavy eyebrows together as he reviews data from my unsuccessful attempt. C'mon, Kion. Don't drag this out. He looks up, almost as if he's heard my internal groan, his broad fingers still moving rapidly over the flat datapad balanced in one large hand. "Serena Jacobs. Failure in the third quadrant." His voice is gruff and raspy, but we've known each other for years, and I recognize the sympathy in the crinkles around his dark eyes. "Get yourself to Medical, ASAP."

"Yes, sir." I bite the words out, hoping my voice won't break with frustration, disappointment, and pain. My raging emotions are begging to release my telepathic power and prove I'm better than the qualification course I've failed. Only the knowing look on my instructor's face—and the calming mantra I've been taught since I was a child—keep them in check. I am separate, I am still. I am separate, I am still. The mantra urges me to keep my power dormant inside my skin, divided from the atmosphere. But the disappointment and the pain make the effort of controlling myself too much. Even with the meditative phrase, my telekinesis thrums around me, filling the air with an electric tension.

Right now, if I was outside the protective steel of ARC headquarters, I'd be sending up an unmissable signal. The psionic power I was born with—the ability to affect matter with my mind, and bend it to my will—translates into a staticky feeling radiating from my slight form and smells faintly of ozone. I am close to exploding. The last time I lost control and let the power burst out of me, it took weeks to beat the dents out of the metal furniture I smashed against the walls. The day they took my brother. And the day when I go after them is pulled farther away from me. Forcing myself to relax, I deliberately deepen my breathing and drop my shoulders. Separate, still. Argh. Just let me out of here! Why are you still talking?

"You can try again in thirty days. Work hard, trainee; I'm sure you'll pass next time. Your session report will be on ARCnet in two hours." My cheeks heat at the implication I haven't worked hard enough and I bristle.

"She cheated!" The words spill out of my mouth before I can swallow them, and the lights above flicker erratically, one of them blowing out with a loud pop. The sound makes me flinch. I'm losing the battle against my storming emotions, breaking protocol by using my powers inadvertently. Like a child. Oh shit.

I look at the floor and clench my fists, purple bruising showing starkly against knuckles white with pressure, and the pain helps me regain focus. The lighting steadies back to its usual level, minus the exploded bulb. The ARC deputy commander frowns at me, but I know him too well to be afraid, even if he does look furious. Straightening my stance, I wince as my leg protests the movement and wait for his judgment. Though if he wants me to do labor, he's gonna have to wait until the medicos clear me. Always a fidget, I hope he knows it's pain—not childishness—making me wriggle when I have to shift my weight again, unable to hold the attentive pose.

He sighs and rakes shoulder-length dreadlocks behind his ears, then rubs his stubbly face as though he's exhausted. "You're arrogant. Part of it is my fault, for encouraging you to test so early, but you must learn to keep your emotions under control and stop believing you're better than everyone else. You're powerful, yes, but we couldn't trust you on a mission now, even if you did pass. You'll see Johan every day this month for extra classes, and when he tells me you've improved, you can try again."

It's one of the longest speeches I've ever heard out of the stoic man's mouth, and I pause in surprise for a moment. Then I realize what he's said, and scowl. Awesome. Not only is my injured leg threatening to collapse under me, but now I've racked up another set of punishment classes. Johan, the main recruit trainer, is a bully—punishment duties, extra work, physical pain—you name it. "Life skills," he calls his teaching methods. Torture, more like it.

Next week is gonna suck. I've already scored recycling duty for "backchatting" one of my teachers. Just 'cause I pointed out an obvious error in his lesson, I have to haul plastics all week? He should be doing it for being an idiot. And now this! Kion's weathered face softens slightly, but I refuse to meet his eyes. I don't want his pity. It doesn't matter if he feels bad for me—I failed. It's his job to make sure operatives are ready for the reality of a world where telepaths are hunted as soon as they set foot outside the safety of their headquarters, meaning right now he can't be on my side. I get it. But it still bites.

He flicks his fingers, and my kit bag rises into the air, hovering next to me in unspoken dismissal until I obediently fasten a mental grip around it. Only then does he release his hold. Glowering, I pull at it telekinetically so it follows in my wake as I hobble away. My power and control are still volatile, though. My emotional and physical distress is making my concentration waver so the bag jerks in the air as it moves after me. I'm too upset to care. I trudge out of the gloomy Arena, leaving its replica streets and alleys behind me, and deliberately avoid looking up at the lanky girl who unfolds from the wall next to the road. The same road where I was writhing in pain just minutes before.

I don't head to Medical. I know I need to, eventually, but I can't face anyone else. Or perhaps I don't really feel like obeying orders. I take the long way around the back of the squat training block, so I don't have to pass the crowded mess hall. The five-minute walk back to the small dorm room I share with two other teenage girls seems to take weeks. It also lasts about ten minutes longer than it should.

The metal corridors echo with footsteps, but I manage to avoid bumping into anyone by taking short sojourns in convenient storage units or empty rooms. By the time I finally limp through my door, I'm almost hopping, unable to put weight on my injured leg. I carefully strip off my black shocksuit, trying not to flinch, and Young Shannon gives me a sympathetic smile. I flop angrily, but carefully, onto my bunk.

"Better luck next time," my other bunkmate, Jue, mutters in a voice not totally devoid of sincerity. The two sidle out the door, leaving me in peace with my defeat, and I watch them go without responding. The three of us are on friendly enough terms, but mostly we were thrown together by circumstance. Honestly speaking, I won't be sorry to see the last of them. If I'd passed the Arena today, I'd be jubilantly moving my meager possessions over to the rowdy chaos of the Barracks right now, instead of lying here stewing in the wake of two girls I have nothing in common with.

My friends are older and have already graded up—or, as today has revealed, betrayed me in favor of keeping status as the youngest ever operative to pass the Arena. But my dormmates know I don't want to be here. Moreover, they know I have little patience for their obsession with romance. I snort as my eyes land on Jue's holo-image of Gav Belias, one of the handsomer heroes of the City Watch. Oooh, what a hunk. I just want to grow up and marry him. Blech. His sparkling, honey-brown eyes and slight, secretive grin are mocking me, and in a fit of pique, I twitch a finger at the holo, sending my telekinetic "muscles" lashing out.

The picture flickers and then disappears, leaving the dark gray wall blank but for the fat vertical stripes of texture—typical of the shipping containers making up most of headquarters. Regretting it immediately, I twist my mouth to one side, hoping I didn't break the little machine—one of the only personal possessions in the room—then shrug. I'll check it later and buy a new one if I did; I have enough credits saved up in commissary. I'm in an awful mood, but it's not Jue's fault. Even if the girl does have terrible taste for slack-jawed idiots with dimples deep enough to lose a fingertip in.

I still can't believe I failed the Arena. Shot in the arse, at that! I groan and drop my chin heavily onto my chest, the thin material of my undershirt sticking to my sweaty skin. I'll be the laughing stock of ARC, and traitorous Abial—my *best friend*—will probably be leading the crowd.

All this time, helping each other through lessons, working together on projects...and apparently status is actually more important than ten years of friendship. Important enough to exploit intimate knowledge about me—the knowledge of my defenses—to mess up the biggest day of my life. I am the best tactical student ARC has ever had. According to the scores, anyway. But it's not translating. I've successfully run the Arena an unheard-of four times in training sessions and completed my first trial run before I even turned fifteen. Nobody else works as hard as I do, especially no one as young. Abial's the only person who even came close.

When it comes to the operative test, though, everything goes wrong. Repeatedly. Maybe having to face an entire team of trained operatives is a bit different from practicing with other students, a little voice in my head whispers. I scowl.

All the extra time I've dedicated to studying, meditating, practicing, and I've messed up again. A trap—a single powerful image, projected by someone who knows my biggest weakness—made me falter. I dropped my mental shields for a split second and the rubber bullets smashed into my side, lifting me off my feet and sending me flying. Crushing my hopes of getting my operative's pips—the badge marking me as a soldier and showing I can be trusted to leave the safety of ARC headquarters. And pushing back the day when I finally go after my missing brother with the equipment and support I know I need.

Those things can only come from ARC. ARC, the Anti—Reprogramming Collective, is the one thing fighting the insidious hold of the government agency known as the Institute. In a world fraught with danger for someone like me—a Psionic, possessing telepathic powers—only ARC is safe. Originally formed by accident when three telepaths on the run banded together, and now a sprawling underground community, ARC is kept secure by thick steel and operatives trained to hide their powers while they forage and purloin necessary supplies. They are the resistance. A single hope in the fight against the Institute. But for me, safety isn't enough. Hiding while the Institute uses Psionics—uses *my brother*—to gather military intelligence, to hunt and find those who would rebel. Uses them to kill. I can't simply wait and do nothing.

The driving force in my life is the knowledge that my baby brother is lost, and I won't stop looking for him until I succeed or die in the attempt. Once I become an operative, I'll have proven I can go out into the world without bringing the full rage of the Institute to bear on us. Then, and only then, will I be able to ask for a team, to propose a mission. To go after Damon with armor, and weapons, and other warriors.

I press a scraped hand to the raw meat-colored bruising mottling the back of my hip and thigh, visible even through my white undershorts. The flesh is hot, swollen, and throbbing so badly I swear I almost see it pulsing with my heartbeat. Sighing, I input a request for a cold pack and wait for the automatic vacuum tube system to drop it into the locker by my feet.

Moments later, a dull thunk lets me know it's arrived. I wriggle around on my thin foam mattress to grab it and hold it gently against the worst of the bruising, hissing as it makes contact. Three bullets connected in almost the same spot, and the ugly mark they left resembles a three-petaled flower, each petal the size of a fist. But the cold seeps into my muscle and numbs the bone-deep injury, cooling my still-sparking temper as well.

The attack was unfair, but in the Arena, failure is failure. Even though no one out in the real world could do what Abial did. I flinch away from thinking about the broken form of my baby brother—a manufactured picture designed to shock and hurt. An image that only worked because Abial had known how to send it. Outside, on a mission, there's no way anyone could be familiar enough with my telepathic frequencies to penetrate my mental defenses. Or know me well enough to project such an effectively debilitating image. But Abial knew how because we'd practiced together for so long. And she'd used it against me, sneaking a vicious thought needle through my protections.

Showing me the thing I feared most: my baby brother, bruised and broken. Unsaveable. Dead.

Once I had wavered, distracted, another operative's slashing thoughtform—a mental weapon as effective as any physical spear—ripped my concentration to shreds. My psionic protection, the invisible but solid bubble surrounding me to cushion blows, was destroyed. So instead of going around my running body, the plastic bullets used in the Arena had slammed into me. If the training gun had been a Zap, one of the energy weapons used by the Institute, I'd be dead, bled out from a pulverized artery and shattered femur. I clench my jaw, anger closing my throat. I turned sixteen seven weeks ago. No one is even allowed to try until they're sixteen, and then only if they've completed all the preliminary courses.

I've gone into the Arena twice now, and my second attempt—today—was thwarted by the very girl who'd been my training companion for my entire life. Abial, who passed the Arena at the age of sixteen and five months, after two unsuccessful attempts, making her the youngest qualified operative ever. We'd iced each other's hard-to-reach bruises, stretched cramping muscles and beaten each other bloody with good-natured smiles. We'd grown up together, pitting ourselves against one another and working as a team to hone our skills. Throughout childhood and into adolescence, we were the closest trainees in age and skill and thus pushed together. Even back when neither of us wanted to be actual soldiers and were training due to the requirement for every Psionic at ARC, we were at least friends. I'd thought maybe we'd be more, for a while.

Two years ago, when Damon was taken in the same raid that nearly killed Abial, everything changed. Now, instead of needing to qualify just so we'd be allowed outside unsupervised, rather than being forced to remain underground for our own safety, we both wanted to be part of the bigger picture. We want vengeance for our pain. We want to join the ranks of the ARC operatives who fought. And so, working together, we'd learned more and faster than anyone had before us. Gotten closer than I'd ever been with anybody.

But everything between us is finished. It was finished when Abial volunteered to go against me during my test. And I feel like an idiot for not suspecting anything. For thinking Abial was only competing because we always did. I can't figure out why she did it. Could the need to hold on to her status as the youngest Arena success be the only reason?

Had it led Abial to betray me in the most personal and cruel fashion possible? Or could there be more? The thought memory of my baby brother's crumpled body jumps back into my mind. It's too much to bear, and I dig my fingers into my bruised thigh. The pain blots out the fake image Abial slipped through my defenses, and I sigh, adjusting myself on the bed.

I want to remember Damon as he was: playful, silly, and kind. He always knew when I needed a hug, and when I wanted to be left alone. He never made me feel as if I had to put on a front, even though he was just a kid. Now, when I have one of my frequent nightmares, there's no small, squirming body climbing into bed to give me a cuddle before I even wake. No little hand to hold mine and tell me it's all gonna be okay, in the utterly self-possessed way he'd had ever since he started talking. One of the benefits of being a Psionic is the truly intimate emotional links we form with people; especially talented Readers like my brother. He knew me inside out. He would understand, even now. He'd understand why I need to fight.

I'm strong but small; small enough that the idea of me being a soldier would be ludicrous to anyone not in the know, which is most of the world. But here, at ARC, physical size is irrelevant. The power we wield and the control we have over it are all that count. Mastery of our Talent takes years of hard practice, but I work harder than anyone. Up at dawn, physical training in the gym, tactical training, and school on top of it all. I've barely breathed for years. As the daughter of the man who leads ARC, a lot of eyes are on me. But that's never mattered.

Damon will be seven now, if he's still alive. I haven't seen him in two years. An ARC team caught sight of him over a year ago but was overwhelmed by the Institute soldiers guarding him and had to retreat. I wish I'd never watched the vid from the operative's helmets. My newer nightmares are of the moment my brother's eyes landed on the slender figure of our father as he held the soldiers back with his psionic powers while struggling to reach his young son.

Instead of showing recognition or hope, Damon's soft, childish face had remained blank and unanimated. Empty. The brown eyes, which had always lit up when his dad entered the room, looked right through him, like he was a stranger. The memory chills me to the bone, and I move the ice pack away as though it's the cause of my pebbling flesh.

That's what the Institute does. They take young telepaths away and wipe them out so the organization can use their gifts as tools. The Institute abducts whoever is found; anyone Talented and unlucky enough to be born inside a major City is usually captured at birth. Even in the rambling and dilapidated townships, telepaths are lucky to avoid their hunters for long. A few of the slum dwellings are made from old shipping containers, and the metal helps hide psionic signals. Some escape. But if someone gets on the radar, they'll stop at nothing to track them.

ARC tries to fight. To take back the stolen and rehabilitate them, help them learn tricks to protect themselves and stay safe. After, they do what they want. Leave, if that's what they desire, or stay and join the fight. The fight I'm desperate to join.

Closing my eyes, I try to shut out the memories and the overwhelming feeling as though I've let my baby brother down, again, the same as the day he was taken. I stay on the bed for an hour or so before the unrelenting pain drives me through the annoyingly sympathetic company of ARC headquarters to the Medical Bay. By the time the third active operative, his insignia shining on mismatched civilian clothing, has slapped me supportively on the shoulder, I'm holding back the urge to deck someone.

Trying not to show how much my leg is hurting, I limp miserably into the Med Bay for treatment. It's a slow day, and they soon have me relaxing under a ray to break up the bruising. After watching the buzzing green line move over my skin for a while, I close my eyes and, bored, meditate. I carefully gather my power and shape it, filling myself with the crackling energy that belongs to me. Meditation is part of the everyday routine for a Psionic. Controlling our power—harnessing it and bending it to our will—we've all learned in training. Much of my education has been in this tamping down, which helps me to keep my power ready to use when I need it, but not involuntarily.

After my scene at the Arena, I definitely need to get a better handle on the link between my power and my emotional state. I breathe in and out as regularly as clockwork, working at it until the friendly nurse approaches to tell me I can go.

My leg feels much better, and I've cheered up enough to join my bunkmates at their table in the mess hall, taking their gentle teasing as good-naturedly as I can when I get there. ARC recruits are warriors in training and expected to hold our tempers and suck it up. Of course, I've always struggled with keeping my hot temper under wraps. And thinking about what happened—what led to my injury—is only gonna make things worse.

Instead of revisiting my failure over and over, I decide to focus on the future. I've got a month to get ready. Next month, I'll get it right. Next month, my shield will be flawless; attacks will slide over it like water over glass. Next month, I'll become an operative. I scan the room and fasten on the avatar of my defeat.

Abial is sitting with Ria and Daine, two respected operatives. Usually she would have been at the end of this table with the rest of her year mates. Either she's deliberately separating herself from the "kids," or she's rubbing her elevated status in my face. Or, maybe, I mentally concede, Abial is too ashamed to try to join us. It's a good thing since I can't guarantee Abial doesn't have a swift punch to the face waiting in her near future. It's always a safe bet to aim blows above the neck, as Abial has sucked at shielding her face ever since we were kids, when we were first learning to build an invisible wall around our bodies. Normally, it would be out of bounds to use personal information. But since Abial already broke one of the unspoken rules of psionic combat by using knowledge of my shielding frequencies against her, I'd be justified. What Abial did was a violation of trust. A kind of emotional assault, made worse by the fact it was done to hurt, to cause me to fail.

I stare at Abial until the other girl meets my gaze. Half of me wishing for something I understand—an apology, an explanation. Anything to justify how my closest friend could turn on me and block my only path to my brother. But Abial only twitches an eyebrow, a placid expression on her broad, brown face. I stifle a growl and narrow my eyes.

I mouth "next time," and grin when Abial blinks and looks away. Jue nudges me gently in the side with an elbow. "You could fix global warming with a stare that cold. We'll put you outside to look at the sun! Oh presto, problem solved!" Shannon snickers, and I force myself to relax a little, digging into my food with sudden gusto.

# Part Two

# Sam

A HEAD FULL of cotton. Angry cotton. Cotton burrowing its way out through my eye sockets and filling the room. A cracking, painful sound, crunching in my throat. Cold thing pressed against my throbbing left temple. I try to roll a little to press more of my overheated skin against the welcome cool, and a pain like I've never experienced before bursts behind my eyes, a planet exploding and plunging me back into oblivion.

I REMEMBER THE sensation next time my brain crawls to consciousness, and wonder if someone electrocuted me or hit me with a Zap gun set to low. I lie as still as I can, which is pretty still at this given time. Usually I'm full of energy, always tapping, fidgeting, twitching. But my limbs appear to be made of concrete now, strangely heavy and impossible to move. I'm lying flat on my back with my head twisted sideways. I don't want to open my eyes in case it kills me, but gradually the fog clouding my thoughts lifts a little.

Staying still appears to be a good strategy. Whatever hit me the first time I woke is by far the worst sensation I've ever experienced. It soon starts to grate on me, though. Not opening my eyes is unbearable, and the need to know what's happening chews me up. When my mind is clear enough, I automatically try to access my power, to feel out the area using the electric wires in the walls, and Wi-Fi signals rebounding off surfaces. To give myself a sort of 3D layout plan.

But my gift is weak and flickering, an injured animal curled in my chest. I gasp. It's never felt like this before, and it terrifies me. I've overextended myself in the past, sure, emptied out my Talent, but I've barely used it today, let alone here in the lab! Why is it so small and feeble?

I give up trying and take stock of my body. My arms and legs are leaden. I tense the muscles, but they won't move enough to lift them away from the surface I'm lying on. Clarity returning slowly, I think I must be restrained. It's not that I can't move my limbs, but they're being held in place. Something tight is cutting into me at my wrists, elbows, thighs, and ankles. My body aches all over, but my head is the worst. Even thinking about moving it sends warning spikes of pain racing through my nerve endings, which feel raw and flayed.

And so I lie still, trapped.

Terror presses in on me, shallowing my breath and leaving me light-headed until I force myself to inhale properly, concentrating on not freaking out and struggling against the bonds. I don't want to draw attention.

Time crawls past, dragging its long fingers over me and daring me to move. Breathing hurts; the bones of my back and hips burn from being pressed stationary against a surface. There's a strange sensation in my left elbow. Eventually, I can't stand it any longer and open my eyes slightly.

The violent light attacks my pupils, even with my eyes squinted almost shut against the whiteness. I adjust slowly, but nothing hits me while I do, and the panic gnawing at my bones recedes slightly. In front of me, I see the glowing tiles, common to many a clinic. Instead of one or two light bulbs, these tiles mean the ceilings and walls give out an even radiance. It's normally quite pleasant. Right now it's like being stabbed in the face. I'm so weak. Why am I so weak? Panic floods me with ice again, stomach prickling and spots dancing in front of my eyes. What's wrong with me?

Maybe I was electrocuted when I tried to move. With my powers out of play, my body wouldn't be able to moderate a Taser blast, and it would hit me like a regular person.

Helpless and trapped, fading in and out, I wait. I'm not sure how long I lie there, but no one comes, and after an eternity, my power begins to return. Slowly—so slowly—I'm able to get a sense of what is around me. The different "feelings" of the signals passing through air and the various materials they hit let me build the shape of where I am. I close my eyes and will my gift to cooperate. Soon, I know I'm lying to the side of a room, not quite against the wall. I'm facing an unmarked, undisturbed-by-furniture wall. The door is down near my feet, and above my head are tables holding various items. There's a computer. I gather my power slowly, carefully, and reach out for the machine.

The urge to jump into cyberspace, leave my useless flesh bag behind me to accept whatever punishment is going to come, is extreme. Get my consciousness to safety, and leave my body behind. That's a last resort, though. Life without physical sensation is weird and timeless. I lost myself for weeks once, coming back to find my body emaciated and my mother frantic. Besides, they might have ways of pulling me back.

I focus on what I'm doing rather than the idea of their control, and the pathetic ghost of my usual Talent connects me to the streams of data pulsing in and out of the clinic. Suddenly my heart freezes. I'm not in the clinic anymore.

And according to the information streaming around me, I've been here for weeks. This is an Institute facility. The Institute.

The shock of it throws my connection off, and it snaps back to my body, trembling in instinctive fear. My breath comes in short, harsh little pants, and my vision swims. I allow myself a few moments of abject panic and despair and grit my teeth. I have to get out of here. But how? I focus my weakened Talent again and seek out more signals.

The buzz of comm units and datapads places me next to a busy corridor, people constantly walking past. There's no information going out connected to me right now, as far as I can tell, in my befuddled state, so I skip back to the computer, looking for knowledge. Where am I? What do they know about me? I find a file marked "DOVZHENKO" and dive into it. This is where I'll find what I need. I hope. What they have on me, what they're holding me for, what they mean to do with me...how the hell I might get out of it. If they have weaknesses I can exploit, this is where I'll find them. The data dump is big, but I scan through it, looking for the important parts. And two pieces of information stand out.

Mother: Apprehended.
Status: Online.

They have my mother. The anger fills me with strength and then power. I'll pay for it later, but for now, my full Talent fills me, accessible for the first time since I woke up. The restraints they placed on me are electronic, incredibly amusing if I wasn't absolutely terrified. They don't understand me—a huge advantage. It means they don't know what I am. What I'm capable of. They must have noticed my slipup but assumed the lights flickered from some sort of normal psionic interaction. That kind of thing happens when Psionics lose emotional control.

But they don't know I can control signals, jump into electronic circuits. They can't or I wouldn't be restrained with things I can command.

My gift buzzing in my veins, I quickly signal approval to the electric cuffs holding me, and after a second, they click open, metal curves finally loose. I heave myself upright with pure force of will, take a second to grit my teeth and swallow bile as I pull the tubing out of my elbow, and open my mind up to the streams of subvisual data.

The second piece of information still nags at me. Status: Online. What does it mean? They're saying I'm online? But the thumb chip doesn't have that sort of heft—it doesn't connect wirelessly to the outside world, and I don't have any other tech on me. So how could I be online?

The persistent throb in my head makes it hard to concentrate, and I reach up to rub the tight muscles in the back of my neck, hoping to relieve the headache, at least for a moment. My hand hits material, not hair. Little threads of cotton catch on the rough skin of my fingertips and another wave of pain makes my stomach curdle. I bend over, coughing, head between my knees, convinced I'm about to vomit. I'm still putting the pieces together as I pant.

Status: Online. My head, wrapped in gauze. Status: Online. Then I realize what it means. They've cut my head open and put in their chips meant to translate telepathy to a visible output on a computer bank. To process the brain waves corresponding to my Talent and interrupt them. Redirect them.

Oh nuke, I know why I'm awake. The chips got brought online, and they must have jumpstarted me. Nausea swamps me, threatening to send me back into unconsciousness. I fight back the tide of blackness dulling my vision and manage to refrain from throwing up. I don't have time for this. Clenching my fists so tightly my knuckles creak in protest, nails digging into the soft flesh of my palm, I push back against the pain.

A cursory scan of my own head leaves no doubt about it. I've been chipped. Tagged like an animal, marked as property. I quickly scan the electronic markers they've pressed into me. I'm pretty sure they're only interpreting electrical signals from my brain and relaying them to a computer. It doesn't feel as though they're using a two-way connection—one they are using to output, program me. With a minor application of gift, I ensure the chips will continue to tell their masters I'm right here, in this room, and nothing unusual is happening. I pause, waiting for a reaction, and hold my breath.

But their chips can't be in tune with my kind of power at all. Else I'd have had people on me as soon as I opened the cuffs they clipped me with. If so, they don't know I'm a technopath; they don't know what I can do. Maybe they've never come across someone like me before. Good news, if anything can be considered good right now. But they have my mother, I remind myself; they could be doing anything to her.

I remember her talking to me seriously once, after a narrow brush with a Reader—one who seemed unusually attuned to the world around her. She was a skinny little thing with a horrible deadness in her eyes. I shiver just recalling the expression on her face. She *knew* what they were doing to her.

My mom told me if I ever got caught, really caught, I should run. Forget about her, forget about everything and run. Head into the slums. The thought of leaving her behind cripples me, but I don't even know where she is. Until I think of a plan. Get out first, then get into their systems properly and find out. Step one has to be getting out of here. As soon as they figure out what I am, I'm done. No second chances. After all, my Talent is useless against a physical attack. Worse than useless, sometimes. If I'm parsing the signals, I might miss what's going on around my body. And it's my body I have to save, or face life as a ghost in a machine. If I'm going to get out of here, I have to stay focused, stay present.

My head pounds, my legs are weak, and my whole body is sweaty and sluggish, but I have to go now. Shuffling to the edge of the bed, I lower my feet carefully to the floor realizing, as soon as they touch the cold surface, my shoes are gone. They weren't good shoes, but they were a damn sight better than no shoes, and I'm already at a huge disadvantage. They haven't even left me my clothes. I'm in a pale gray fiberpaper smock. All the better for nuked-up doctors to violate your flesh in.

My throbbing head makes my vision waver with every beat, and when I stand, I immediately stumble. I manage to catch myself by grabbing onto the edge of the gurney with both hands, but I feel my head bobbing—a swimming motion like I can't really hold the weight of my own skull. I refuse it, shove the weakness back where it can mewl and whimper and sway all it wants. I will die if I stay here.

Worse. They will take everything that makes me *me*— every memory of who I am and what formed me—and wipe it clean. I know the stories. I've had nightmares about what I've found online, hidden deep in their safest virtual vaults.

I will be an empty, hopeless android, waiting for my next instruction.

And I refuse.

It's amazing what you can force your body to do in a crisis. The pure adrenaline of utter fear pushes me to the door. My sweaty palm can't get traction on the door sensor for a moment, but once it does, it only takes me a split second to splice the code from the last scan and plug it back in. To convince the electronic reader I am Dr. Sheridan, whoever they may be. The last entrant to this room, at any rate.

As the door slides back, I clench my jaw and thrust my Talent outward, hitting every piece of technology I can. I reckon my blast radius is about a hundred meters on a good day, but this is not a good day.

But one great thing about electricity is it works in circuits. If I break the circuit here, it will affect a much larger area. I hate the dark, but right now, I need the cover. It's my only shot.

Pow. The lights snap off, bulbs blowing with fizzing pops behind every panel. Nice and expensive to fix, I think vindictively as I stagger into the pitch-black corridor. Around me, people yell, trying to use their datapads and comms to illuminate the space. No good. I fried them too. EMP boy, that's me. I press my hand to the wall, using a sort of wire-frame vision, reading the wireless signals still bouncing around to create a 3D representation of what's around me.

The people are hard to avoid, though; with their tech dead and useless, I can't "see" them and bump into them on occasion, moving as fast as I am. I try not to groan and hope nobody grabs onto my obviously-not-a-doctor-smock. But the panicking people who can feel my physical body are the least of my worries.

Anyone telepathically scanning the crowd would realize who I am in a split second.

The place will be swarming with Readers, and I have no way of knowing who is and who isn't, so my best bet is to put as much space as possible between me and the whole place. Hopefully, they'll be too busy attempting to get some sort of communications up and running again to notice me.

The pitch-black is totally disorientating, but I stay in the middle of the corridor, reasoning since every instinct is screaming at me to press against the wall surely everyone else will be out of the way. Harsh breathing surrounds me, shouts and yells, thudding footsteps. Suddenly, my bare foot is stomped on by an overzealous runner, and I curse loudly, unable to keep it in as the bones bend.

Someone grabs me by the shoulder, slams my body back against the wall. Tensing all the muscles in my neck just about stops my injured head from connecting, and I bring my knee up as hard as possible. I'm lucky and connect well enough to make my attacker grunt in pain and release me. I didn't hit anything squishy, though; my knee is actually bruised from impact.

Unfortunately, it's the same leg that just had its foot stomped on. I flinch as I put my weight on it, but manage to get moving, albeit at a slow, staggering pace. I make it through two sets of doors, thankfully stuck open when my power hit. If they'd been shut, I'd really have screwed myself. I round a corner, and the blackness lightens until I make out lights—the edge of my power cut. Shit.

I push a second power surge through the building, but it scrapes the barrel of my energy and leaves me coughing flecks of vomit onto the floor between my feet. Usually my gift comes so easily, but now it hurts, and my body is physically rebelling—the equivalent of shouting poison, poison! I force the power through and the lights flicker out.

I bounce off the wall, rebound off a person, and eventually stagger into someplace that I think is a control center, judging by the amount of wiring ending here. My head spinning, I collapse onto the floor, desperately hoping there's no one present since the equipment is fried. It's quiet in the room, all the noise coming from pounding feet and the occasional shout outside, although the furor is dying down. I imagine everyone's trying to get out of the dead zone I created.

I curl up, shaking, my muscles in a sort of spasm. Gradually my breathing slows, and my body relaxes. Several minutes pass without me getting shot, so I think I've made a good decision dodging into the room. Then I throw up again, although there's nothing in my stomach, so it's more of a helpless, miserable dry heaving on all fours. Eventually, I force myself to crawl forward.

My hand bumps into something that moves when I touch it—a rolling chair, I realize, after a moment of sheer panic. I use it to haul myself up and crumple into it, leaning my head back carefully so the surgical site doesn't connect with anything. Closing my eyes, I push my recalcitrant Talent out, hopelessly searching for a plan. Can I head back into the corridor and try to find a way out? I doubt I have enough energy left to push out another pulse, but I might be able to click a lock or two.

Regardless, I don't have much time. Without shoes, my feet will have left thought-traces stamped into the floor tiles, vividly marking my route for anyone with half an ounce of sense. The only thing I have going for me is the chance of them immediately realizing I cut the power is pretty low. They'll be wondering why the backup generators aren't working; they'll have to search the area with flashlights. They'll have no idea who's missing from where until they manage to sort the chaos out. For a normal Psionic, the only way to even get out of the first room would have been a brute force attack, slamming the door right out of its frame. Obviously, I didn't bust anything down. If they don't connect me to the power outages, they might think they're being invaded, letting me slip away undetected or at least buying me time. I hope.

I scan the room for any working tech, but everything was too close to my blast radius and is totally blown out. So I can't conveniently download a map of the building. I squeeze my fists tightly, and my power flickers and dies. It's going to be a hands-on sort of day—I'm totally drained. Which leaves mundane options. My mind churns over what I know. If we're in an Institute lab, we're underground, so everything has to go in and out. People through doors, but electricity through laid cables, and air...air through ducts! Lit up with my idea, I stumble to my feet, cursing under my breath when my injured leg wobbles. I scramble over to the equipment lining the walls, now dark and useless. Above it, I hear the faint hissing of the ducts. The air system no doubt has multiple fail-safes and is designed to automatically reroute in case of shutdown, meaning it's still running so we don't all suffocate.

At five foot six, I'm definitely not the tallest guy in the world, and even when I get up onto the desk, the air vent at the top of the wall is at the limit of my reach. I wrestle with the screws, trying in vain to get my fingernails under them. I slip a few times, slicing my skin. But after a few terrifying minutes, I have three of them loosened.

I don't have time to put the chair back in its original location, so I say a silent prayer no one will notice, wipe the bloody smears off the wall as best I can in total darkness, and quickly swing the vent around so it's turned up above the hole, connected by one corner. A top corner. I should be able to pull it closed from inside, and if I take the screws with me, it's possible no one will figure out where I've gone, at a glance. I mean, as soon as they have a Reader in the room they'll be after me like hunting hounds, but there's no point in taking chances.

Climbing up through the small vent is one of the hardest things I've ever done. Thanking Google and malnourishment for my scrawny frame, I sort of jump and thrust my arms in, locking my hands around my wrists and shoving my elbows out so they wedge against the sides of the duct. I then have to scrabble my toes against the wall, wiggling farther in, inch by inch. My entire chest is scraped raw and bruised by the time my feet are inside, and then I realize I've made a mistake.

I'm stuck facing forward, which is surely the only way to make any progress, but there's no room for me to wiggle around and shut the vent behind me. Nuke, nuking nuke! Idiot. There's no turning back; it's literally impossible, and I'm thinking there's no solution when I hear a scraping sound behind me. Crushing myself against the side of the duct, I turn my head, and I see I've had a huge stroke of luck. Behind me, the vent cover has slid down, twisting on its single remaining screw. It's mostly covered the entrance. Not totally, but it's going to be a lot less noticeable than a gaping maw on the wall when the lights come back on.

Reluctant to waste any more time, I start crawling forward. It's unbelievably loud, my bones colliding with metal to propel me forward, and I think it'll be a miracle if I don't get shot right through the vent casing. I can't hear anything but my own clanging progress and am completely disoriented until I find myself crawling parallel to a trunk of cables lashed together with plastic ties. Wrapping my trembling hand around the plastic insulation, I tune in to the latent charge in the wires, looking for their destinations. I'm just about able to sort out their purposes and start to worm my way forward, taking as close a route as possible to the main air intake whenever there's a junction, hoping against hope it will lead me to the outside world.

The hellish nightmare crawl blurs into a swirl of bruises and terror. The base of my skull sends out unrelenting waves of pain. I catch myself fading into unconsciousness, convinced I'm still moving and realizing moments later I have pins and needles in my arm from lying on it. I'm on the verge of tears—the hot kind that burrow out directly from your heart. My eyes are stinging, painful, like the salt rimming them is too strong even for the body that made it, and I sniff, a wet sound in the darkness.

I want my mom. I want to wake up and realize all of this is a horrible nightmare. This morning, I got out of bed to a breakfast of thin porridge and sauntered to school. I handed in a project, wrote a paper, tried not to fall asleep in math class, and then made my way to my biannual checkup. Now I'm crawling through an air duct, on the run from people who want to cut my personality out of me as if it were a tumor, so they can use what remains for their own purposes. I'll have three of their chips in my brain—electronic ticks *buried* in my flesh—for the rest of my life. Sure, I can keep them from doing their job, but a part of them is inside me, never to be removed, and it's disgusting.

I can't believe no one has found me yet, but it's possible they don't even know I'm gone, thanks to the chips. I wonder if they had cameras in the room they left me in. If they did, and the servers were far enough away from the blast zone, they might find images of me hacking the lock, I was too out of it to think about it at the time. I keep crawling. Nothing to be done now.

I have absolutely no idea how much time has passed when I start to hear the whump, whump of machinery. The passage is colder, waking me up a bit, and I manage to pick up the pace a little, inspired by the possibility of an end to the claustrophobic tunnel. The air begins to press against me; it trails through my sweat-soaked hair and across the hypersensitive area covered with the bandage. Normally they tattoo their slaves, and I grimace at the thought.

Hopefully, the tattoo comes after the chips, not simultaneously. I hate the idea of being visibly marked. At least the chips can be a secret, and once I'm sure I've disabled them, I can try to forget about them.

When I finally make it to the massive turbine, the noise is so extreme it permeates my bones, rattling my skeleton as though a giant has picked me up and is shaking me. I close my eyes to try to adjust—process the noise as temporary and move past it emotionally, but I pass out. When I force my eyelids open, the light has changed. Before, a grayish, foggy source of light allowed me to make out slight detail, whereas now it's pitch-black. I hear the machinery, without being able to make out a single part of it. I feel it forcing the air through the myriad of ducts, but I can't even work out how close it is to me. The facility definitely has the ability to monitor airflow through ductwork, and it's possible there'll be a waiting committee for me on the other end, but there's nothing I can do about it now.

Presumably, just past the spinning blades is the outside world, as the whirling machinery must be sucking air from somewhere open and propelling it into the cavernous building below. All I have to do is get past this murderous contraption to get out.

The crawl out of the duct ends in a graceless tumble to the floor—fortunately only a small drop. Unfolding my aching limbs takes a little time, and rubbing the sensation back into my freezing skin is an experience I hope never to repeat. I try to use my wire-frame vision to get an idea of what's in front of me, but the whirring machinery is disturbing my concentration, so I can't be sure of anything. My brain's not working properly, skipping weirdly. I can't focus.

The room is about eight feet square, one entire wall a huge fan unit pulling air into the system. It's pushing against my body as if I'm caught in a tornado. The noise of the blades is rhythmic, but so loud it's difficult to make sense of it. Blindly, I press my hands against the wall I emerged from and shuffle my way around. I want to see if there's any convenient object I can thrust into the machinery to jam it. With luck, I'll be able to run through while the blades are stopped.

My exploration leads me to a door set into the wall. I almost try the handle and then realize it almost certainly leads back into the Institute. The maintenance crew needs a way in and out, after all, and what are the chances they have unguarded entrances or exits? Tempting, but a last resort I'll only use if there's no way past the fan. I can't wait in here to die.

A stroke of inspiration leaves me padding my fingers around the doorframe at shoulder height, and I whoop under my breath when my fingers catch on a switch. A light switch.

I flick the button, and to my excitement, light floods the room. But it's a lot like being poked in both eyes with something extremely sharp, and I instinctively shut my now-watering eyes in pain. Sadly, the switch doesn't have a dimmer, so I have to wait for my pupils to adjust in small increments, squinting through tear-spangled lashes until I can finally see.

The room is about the size I estimated, maybe a bit bigger. There's no equipment—no shelf I can move and thrust at the fan, no helpful toolbox. I scream in frustration, the noise completely swallowed in the throbbing rattle of the spinning blades. For a few moments, I cycle through wanting to cry, scream some more, kick the wall, or give up and collapse in a corner, waiting to be found. My last thought scares me: the thought of surrendering. I'm a lot of things, but a quitter? I've never been a quitter. Especially when the stakes are this high.

It snaps me out of my cycle. I grit my teeth and allow myself one more huge sniff, then swallow and shake off the crippling self-pity. No more pathetic whining about how unfair it is. The world isn't fair, and it never will be. But I am smart. The Institute thinks they're cleverer than everybody else, got it all figured out, but they don't know me.

Belittling my terrifying enemies in my head makes it more manageable, and I lean my sore shoulders against a metal wall panel, willing my brain to do what it does best— leaps of mechanical intuition.

If I could just make the fan stop for a minute, I realize, I'd be able to think clearly, figure out a way to escape. But how could anyone think with all this noise, all this pressure? I look up at the huge machine, whirring blades thumping air out and slamming it into my body with unbelievable strength. My face creases in a frown at the cabling running up from the center of the fan, linking it to the electric wiring lying thick against the frame of the...

Shit. I'm an idiot. My brain is fried, and I'm not even thinking straight. I fish for my power, looking for enough strength to blow out the fuses in the connection.

But there's nothing. Absolutely nothing. My knees turn to dust instead of bone, and I stagger, falling backward and landing on my unpadded behind in shock. I'm empty, totally drained. The last time this happened was when a kid got hit by an elec-car right in front of me. I was eleven, and I blew out a whole city block, and then I slept for a week before I got my Talent back.

I'm dehydrated, exhausted, and totally powerless. I clambered into the duct, leaving psychic traces everywhere—a clear trail for any Reader to follow. I have nothing left to fight with, and it's only a matter of time before they figure out where I am.

# Serena

"ABIAL, ABIAL, WAIT up." *Abial,* I throw it psionically, as well, loud enough that people in the classroom facing the corridor look up. Abial doesn't reply, striding ahead of me so fast she's gonna disappear around the corner any second. Throwing politeness and protocol out the window, I reach out telekinetically and grab her belt loop gently, the way we used to when we were kids.

The violence of her response astonishes me, and only swift reactions save me from head butting the wall, catching myself with one hand, and by the time I've pushed off, Abial's out of sight. But I trace her; I still know her well enough to pick out the slight buzz of her passing, even with her shields as tight as she can hold them. We were inseparable for years, and I still feel her as if she's family. Linked to me.

She's in the library, head down and headphones on, every line in her body screaming "Leave me alone" when I catch up. But I won't. I drop into the seat opposite her, waiting for her to acknowledge me.

Finally, reluctantly, she raises her eyes, dark and unreadable. Her usually placid—almost smug—expression is heavy and bruised with hard feeling.

"What?" she enunciates violently, but quietly enough to avoid being shushed. Speaking instead of communicating silently makes me flinch back, my feelings bruised. I didn't realize it was possible to hurt even more. Well, if she doesn't want to share her emotions, if she wants to *lie* to me, so be it. I quash the tiny piece of guilt inside telling me I've been lying to her for months, hiding the rush of feelings that started boiling in my stomach when she looked at me with the intensity that colors everything she does. My feelings are my business, not hers, and I've gone out of my way to make sure she never had to know about my stupid, idiotic heart.

"What?" I repeat, sounding kind of hollow and sad to my own ears. For a second, her face softens, and I catch an echo of distress wafting from her, and then she closes back up. She doesn't answer, only stares at me, flat-eyed and tense. I gather my nerve; I forced this confrontation after all. Abial's been doing her level best to avoid me entirely for the past four days. "Why?" I can't find the words to clarify, so I rest my hand palm up on the table, hoping she'll take it, and we can avoid the awkward clumsiness of words.

Her lip curls; she pointedly looks at my hand and then makes fists of her own, resting her knuckles on the table in front of her. "Why?" she repeats, radiating disgust. "Well, I guess I figured since you'd already betrayed me I may as well get even."

My heart does a weird squeezing thing in my chest, but she's already stuffing her sweater into her backpack, clearly about to stalk off.

"Betrayed you?" And I know; I know, suddenly, she's seen what I've been hiding, and she hates me for it.

"You lied—" She spits the words and then pauses and looks me over with disdain clear in her eyes. "—or at least never told me the truth. And you know as well as I do that's just as bad." She leaves me with the last barb lodged in my heart and storms off. This time, I don't try to follow.

THE DAY OF retest crawls toward me, the hours stretching out unbearably. I spend the entire month watching the calendar and training, almost glad of the punishment duties and extra classes keeping me so occupied I don't have too much time to dwell. In fact, I barely have time to sleep. I've taken to eating in my room or the gym; grabbing a foodpack so I don't waste time socializing. Of course, it doesn't hurt that this helps me in the quest to avoid any interaction with my former best friend slash unrequited crush. The only good thing is she appears to agree entirely with my unspoken plan. Apart from when it comes to training with Kion, who runs specialist classes once a week, we barely catch sight of each other. I get used to the feeling of guilt clogging my throat.

Finally, finally, the day dawns. My nerves sing as I pull on my tight-fitting shocksuit. The thin gel pads designed to harden with impact lie flat and snug against my lightly muscled frame. It feels good, a second skin, and surely it's a positive sign. Third time lucky. Isn't that a saying from somewhere? I wonder if my father will show up this time, or if watching me fail the first time was enough. He wasn't there when Abial cheated.

The mission setup will be exactly the same as the last: A team of eight qualified operatives is in charge of the Arena's defenses. My challenge: To make it through the "city." Strength, secrecy, and a combination of the two are all acceptable methods. If I can hide my psionic presence, I might be able to avoid the opposition until the very end. If not, it will come to a telekinetic and physical fight. I just have to get through, by any means necessary.

One of the oldest operatives, Jamal, passed his test by taking a bunch of MREs in with him and holing up. Eventually the hunting team got too hungry to keep looking, and the rules state that once someone is out of the Arena, they can't re-enter. When the operatives left to get food, they were out, and Jamal walked over the finish line in plain sight. They changed the system after him. Now there's a time limit, meaning I'll have only an hour to make it across. An hour to get past whatever hunters are out there, through the streets, and to the other side of the Arena. I bounce on my toes gently, embracing the familiar rush of adrenaline fizzing in my blood. This time, I'm fighting smart. Avoid them, and then they can't hurt me. Hide and run; no heroics, out the other side before time runs out. If they don't find me, no one can do what Abial did.

Suddenly the horn announcing the start of the test blares, and the light over the entrance goes green. I slip into darkness. The defending operatives—those hunting me—will be entering from the other side at the same time. I send out tentative mental feelers, trying to ascertain their positions while keeping my shields prepared for anything. It's a delicate balance and difficult to learn; keeping the invisible layer of protection solid enough to absorb a direct blow, but fluid and ready to whirl bullets away from their intended path.

After checking my defenses, I look up and spot a camera in front of me and a slow grin spreads over my face. I'm ready. Without warning, I leap directly up in the air. It's a two-story jump, which means I have to push my power out through the soles of my feet to send me high enough. I land as quietly and lightly as a leaf on the low surface of the roof, booted feet barely making a whisper against the smooth glass. For realism, the Arena is laid out in an imitation of the City streets. After all, in the City is where operatives are most likely to be in danger. It makes sense for us to be tested in a similar layout. There are several towering buildings, although here in the reproduction, we can't get to the top of those because they disappear into the ceiling after four stories. Some of the buildings, like the one I'm currently crouching on, are lower, wider, and sprawling.

I look down. I make out movement a few streets away and hear scuffing noises to my right, as well as in front of me. My opponents are on the roof. And they're armed. Opponents: that's all they are. The enemy. Not Dom, who taught me to tie my shoes because my father was too busy. Not Laurie, who knows all the best folk songs. Only masked foes, trying to keep me from Damon. Just like the real thing. Hunkering into the shadow at the edge of the building, I close my eyes and slip deeply into the center of my power, imagining the internal light of my Talent filling every cell. My consciousness has to align completely with my physical body so I can be both undetectable and ready to act—a perfect Zen state of awareness I've spent years learning to achieve.

I slide into it, my skin tingling with energy ready to protect or attack as I command it. This is it, this time. No going back. They won't let me out on the streets unless I succeed, so succeed I must. And this is my last chance. If I don't get past the test on my third try, I'll get pushed into intelligence service or worse. I definitely don't have the head to be a teacher. I snort, thinking about trying to get a bunch of kids to listen to me without resorting to dangling them upside down, then sober. I'm gonna make it.

Certainty trickles through my bones, driving away the mild irritant of the armor digging into my hips, and the coldness of the roof seeping into the balls of my feet. It's designed cleverly, and we all hate it because cold saps psionic ability. Cold steel is the worst, leeching the energy right out of us faster than anyone can think. Making the

Arena so cold lowers my chances of completing the course. Better move fast before it weakens me too much. In order to avoid standing out from my surroundings, I make my mental shield as thin and unnoticeable as possible. I tune it to the frequency of the air and stay perfectly still. My defenses are weaker this way, but I'm less likely to be found. Those hunting for me have their own psionic abilities and will use any advantage they can, any sign of me. And even a tiny flaw in the skin of my protection could signal my location—a beacon of power to lead them to their prey. The longer I stay hidden, the better chance I have of making it.

As subtly as possible, I spread my awareness out, pinpointing the locations of the movement I noticed. The operatives' shields are good, but motion displaces air, creates environmental ripples. Tracking those ripples like the threads of a spider in a web, I nod once and form a mental map of my surroundings, complete with moving blips to represent the people who are going to try really hard to shoot me. People die in the Arena if they're not ready. Better than being taken because you were sent out into danger unprepared. Still, dead is dead. But not me, not today. All right, suckers. Bring it on! My movement is explosive. Bursting across the roof faster than a normal human can run, using well-practiced telekinesis to power my feet, I leap into the air.

I land sure-footed on the next roof over, seconds before a mental attack gropes after me. Huge, invisible fingers want to catch hold of my moving figure and pin me. A basic attack. Unsurprised, I fend the operative off, slipping through the thoughtforms without missing a step.

Dropping like a stone into the alley below, I push force downward out of my feet so I bounce into a run up the wall and pack my hands and forearms with telekinetic power, ready to attack with one of my favorite moves. I invented the technique when I was twelve, and around ARC it's called the Serena Slam—a strike where I wrap my bones and sinew in Talent, bracing them and increasing their strength, instead of sending power out in an invisible fist. When he rounds the corner, only inches from me, I smash my fist into his face. Perfect timing. The operative's shields deflect the force of the blow, or I'd have torn his jaw clean off, but the muted power is still enough to cause his eyes to roll up in his head. He slumps to his knees and sideways into a messy heap. One down.

Muted gunfire cracks through the air, making me flinch, and I realize there are already other operatives headed toward me. The first guy must have sent out a telepathic shout. My cover blown, I dash through the shadows, tearing round the corner to take cover as the pellets tatter the air behind me, several spun away by my shield, which I push outward as I sprint. Skintight armor is useless against projectiles, as it can't absorb that much energy directly, but now I have a protective globe surrounding me, and I charge forward, thoughts of stealth mostly forgotten.

I almost run into two more black-clad figures as they close in on me from the gloom, raising their hands for a telekinetic attack. Screaming defiance, I mirror them, searching mentally for the best escape route. They'll drag me out of the air if I leap, so instead, I call my power, let it fill me, and unleash it in a powerful wave, surging forward in its wake. It rushes ahead of me like a tsunami—a moving wall of energy, meant to sweep them out of my way. The operative on my right is so distracted by the brute force approach of my telekinetic attack he fails to react fast enough, and I deliver a sloppy flying roundhouse kick on my way past, my foot slamming into the side of his knee, sending him to the ground. Before I can knock him out, the other attacker is on me from behind. Abial, my awareness tells me as our shields and bodies crash into each other.

I pour everything I have into my skin for protection, not allowing Abial to find a weak point or slide through my barrier with any nasty, distracting surprises. Our powers push against each other as we grapple, each trying to force the other away. Struggling for a grip against the more powerful hands of my larger opponent, I take a chance and jerk my head backward, my skull colliding at top speed with the bridge of Abial's nose.

There's a satisfying crunch, and Abial's grip slips. She always forgets to anchor her shield around her face. Twisting sideways, I hammer at her shields with all my strength, aware of footsteps closing in. Breaking loose, I bend my knees and leap, using Abial's head as a convenient boosting point; the blow sends the other girl to the ground. Unable to suppress a cocky smirk, I dash away across the rooftop, scanning my surroundings.

Rapidly figuring out my new position, I sense movement and twist sharply to the left, barely in time to avoid another spray of bullets whistling past. Two of them clip my shield, sapping more of my strength as I absorb the powerful blows. Nuke! Snipers on the roof. I leap from roof to roof, barely pausing to balance, jinking left and right with preternatural speed and grace to avoid the continuing gunfire. By the time I approach the edge of the building guarding the exit to the Arena, I'm running at full speed. Heartbeat pounding in my ears, I throw myself forward into a handstand and grab the edge of the roof. My momentum carries my legs over the empty space below. As soon as my body is horizontal, I push out from the wall, using telekinesis to guide my body into a perfect gymnast's landing, and sprint flat out for the end of the alley, the end of the test.

Yes! Exultation flows through me, reviving my flagging muscles. The bullets from the left take me completely by surprise, but my shield holds, and I dodge sideways, taking cover in a doorway and breathing through my mouth in an effort to be silent. I trickle awareness out again and discover I'm about fifteen meters from the exit.

Two operatives bracket it, guns and shields held high. Bile rises in my throat. I can't quit, not an option. I'd rather take the bullets and get carried out of here. If I get over the line, they might let me contest the ruling, whether I "died" or not. Depends how many times they hit me. *Nuke,* I swear under my breath, rapidly calculating the odds. Within minutes, the other operatives scattered throughout the course will be on me, called by the noisy weapons or their team's psionic connection. I have to go immediately, or I'll be facing eight strong, well-trained soldiers acting in unison. Well, seven, I correct myself, remembering the unconscious guy who ran right into my superpowered fist.

But I'm weaker now, tired, with my strength and Talent depleted. There's no way I'll make it if I don't go immediately. And this time, I know, I have to make it. I take a moment to center myself and recheck my worn-out shields, then grit my teeth and prepare for the inevitable attack. Zaps bark as soon as I leave the safety of the doorway, but I whip the bullets around my body, using physics to my advantage, and fling them back in the direction of the operatives.

One is taken by surprise, a redirected bullet thudding into him as I power forward at top speed. His loud yell splits the eerie quiet, and the attack from the right peters off. The remaining operative has stepped in front of the door, and his left hand is outstretched, hurling telekinetic power at me. It slows my legs until it's like I'm running through water, a torrent of pure energy pushing at my calves and feet. He's trying to wrap his power around me, grip onto me, but I'm too strong. I fend away his attempts so he can't gain purchase, almost as though I'm bending his mental fingers backward and sliding my legs through the narrowing gaps.

But suddenly the gun in his hand jumps, its muzzle trained on my face. I gather the last dregs of my waning power and push it out, powering from my feet as I leap. It sends me hurtling wildly into the air; I'm at the end of my tether, with very little control left. But the soldier doesn't have time to react and pull his power back from the ground-level stream he sent at my legs. If he hadn't committed so fully, it's possible he could have caught me, or at least padded himself. As it is, he can't. I crash into him, body weight and momentum powering another slam, and he smashes to the ground with me on top of him.

I hastily detangle myself, sensing the approach of more soldiers, but the clumsy landing has twisted my ankle, and I run awkwardly for the exit. My Talent is totally drained; there's not enough left to move a feather. My last jump scraped the barrel dry. But the exit is right there. All I have to do is make it a few more meters. A few more meters are the only thing standing between me and going to find my brother. I can't even keep my head up, and I stumble, careening off a wall. I must be close. So close. Then a sunburst of pain explodes in the small of my back, and I'm catapulted forward, catching myself heavily on my hands, face slamming into the rough concrete floor.

Exhausted, I lie there, my heart breaking in my chest, unable to believe I failed again. Inches away. Not good enough, again. Letting my father down *again*. Sobs catch in my throat, tearing like glass shards. They won't let me try again. That's it. No one to go after Damon, no one who knows him like I do. They'll never find him without me. A soft cry escapes as I press my forehead against the hard ground, unable to get up. Then footsteps approach. I know I should try to drag myself upright, at least retain a semblance of dignity. I can't. I don't care anymore. I see two military-booted feet uncomfortably close to my head, and I roll a little, gasping at the fresh stab of pain lancing into my back.

"Well, if you stay down there you'll have to wait longer to collect your insignia." Kion grins at me and opens his meaty palm, revealing a shiny silver pin.

"Buh...?" I blink at him, confused, and he smirks, hauling me to my feet as easily as if I were a wet kitten. I manage not to cry out in pain.

"You pass. You're through." He can't hide his pleasure at his own words, dark eyes sparkling as he steadies me and pins the ARC operative's badge onto my collar—a silver curve widening at one end, like the trail of a shooting star.

An undignified squeak slips out, and I swallow. "But I got shot! I'm dead!" I try to bat the hand away, convinced he's missed my final failure, unwilling to take the pin representing my life's work, only to have it taken away when he sees the footage replayed. He must not have seen it, somehow. But he rolls his eyes at me, stilling my hands with his telekinesis while he finishes attaching the badge.

"Tech marks you as through the gate when the shot was fired. Bad shoot. Operative Berke wasn't fast enough. Game over. You win." His demeanor remains professional, but I know him, and his eyes are dancing with happiness. Abial. The last shot had been from Abial, but it hadn't counted. Bad shoot. I've passed. My knees almost give out, the spreading ache from my lower back beating in time with the blood whooshing in my ears. "I passed? I passed!" I sound slaphappy, even to my own ears, and so don't complain when a bearded ginger soldier—Marty, I think he's called—slings my arm around his shoulder and drags me off to the medical bay, stabilizing my torso with a telekinetic brace. I don't even bitch about having to lie on my stomach for an hour while they check my spine and run the ray over me. Plastic bullets aren't supposed to break bones, but they hurt like blazes, and I willingly submit to the doctor's orders.

When my father comes to see me, pride and fear are warring in his sleepy hazel eyes. As the leader of ARC, he needs every soldier he can get. As a parent, though, I know he wants to protect me, not put me in danger by sending me out into the world above. He rubs his thumb gently over my ARC insignia, and I can't hide my elation, even in the face of his fear. He congratulates me, anyway, although his voice is sad. He has to be thinking about the possibility of losing a second child. But I know he'll respect my success and the rules of ARC. One of those rules is that, as a qualified operative, I'm eligible for putting together proposals, as well as being given assignments. When I'm medically cleared, he'll assign me my first mission. It could be anything, from stealing a shipment of supplies to feed the families at ARC, to kidnapping and interrogating an Institute soldier. Or, it could be what I long for: the chance to go after one of the children the Institute routinely uses to gather intelligence and quash rebellious thoughts. To go after Damon. The thought of pulling my brother from the clutches of the government agency that tortures him lull me to sleep.

It takes four days for Medical to clear me for duty. Bruising on the spine can cause complications, so it's treated cautiously. The parade of well-wishers has kept me supplied with snacks and treats, though, and my dorm buddies made me a sign saying "Youngest Operative Ever (Eat Rad, Abial)" and hung it above my bed. I see it when I'm finally released to pack up my room, and it cracks me up. It surprises me how nostalgic I am as I pile the last of my meager belongings into boxes. The initial burst of excitement and pride has faded somewhat, leaving a solid sense of determination and calm in its wake. Realistically, I know the chances of being sent on the high-risk mission I want are low. But even if they deny my request to go after my brother, I'll do my best for ARC and prove to them I can be trusted with anything. One day, my chance will come, and I'll be ready.

Finally, boxes at my feet, I sit on the bare mattress and look around the stark room. There's never been much in the way of personal belongings in the room—they're too difficult to obtain—but it looks strange without my chaotic corner of clothes and weapons manuals. I rub my thumb against my brand new operative pin and sigh, getting to my feet, finally out of excuses to continue avoiding what I've been working toward for years. My chest is humming, with nerves or with excitement, I can't tell. The very last thing I do before I pick up my stuff and leave my old bunk is digitally submit a proposal to Ops. The proposal that would send me after Damon, with a small, hand-chosen team. The team is one smaller than a month ago, Abial's name deleted from the request list.

IT'S BEEN TWO weeks since I moved into the Barracks, and I've been doing nothing but training and checking my datapad for an assignment. Working with qualified operatives, including the opportunity to be on the other side of the Arena, keeps me somewhat occupied, but I'm still chafing at the bit, wondering why nothing has come through for me. My new roommate has been out the entire time I've bunked there, meaning I have altogether too much time to myself. Against my wishes, I miss Abial and the companionship we once shared. But I still go out of my way to be anywhere Abial isn't, only speaking to her as much as is necessary, when it can't be avoided. I'm lonely, and sad, and getting more irritable by the day.

When the order finally comes, my comm beeps loudly, jerking me out of a deep slumber. I open the file, and my heart simultaneously drops with disappointment and hammers with adrenaline. There isn't much information, but there's enough for me to know this assignment can't be anything to do with Damon. He was taken here, in Fourth City, and this order tells me to prepare to travel. But anything that hurts the Institute could help him, or at least weaken the hold of the organization, so I read the information twice to commit it to memory before I get ready to head to the Ops department. Right, so... Now it's really real, and it's on me.

My hands are shaking, but not with fear, as I pull on civilian kit. Body armor would never make it through the scanners, which use millimeter wave technology to hunt for suspicious objects, including weapons. I'm going to Second City, which means taking the Intercity tube. So my team is on its own. No reliable backup. ARC might have resources in Second City, but they're limited compared to those of the Institute, who are housed in every one of the eight major settlements. ARC only really has a presence here, in Fourth City. Second City is hundreds of kilometers away, on the other side of the desert. If we're going to Second City, we won't have anywhere to run if we get noticed.

A shiver runs down my spine. Why am I being sent on a dangerous out-of-city mission for my very first assignment? Then I realize. Clean identities aren't hard to come by— there are always forgers working on faking Citizen cards. Any basic clean ID will get someone through the Wall separating the townships from the wealthy. They won't, however, fool the facial recognition software guarding the most secure facilities. This mission needs someone who's never been caught on camera before, so they get through the intense electronic security measures the government installed on the tube. If that's the reason, my partner is likely to be another new operative who hasn't yet been compromised. A recently graduated operative. An operative like Abial. Nuke.

# Part Three

# Sam

I DON'T KNOW how long I cry before I manage to peel myself off the floor. I set my nervous breakdown aside as totally understandable, but not helpful in any way, and something I can return to later, when I'm not literally in the sand wasp's nest. Gritting my teeth, I look around the room again, as though some sort of equipment is going to magically appear to save me.

And then I see it. A large metal switch raised to the "red" position. On. That's what powers will get you. Total idiocy and inability to think like a regular person. The off switch. Of course. There's no way maintenance would be in here without a kill switch. I stagger over to it, yanking it downward before I've thought through my actions. The handle grates, catches, and snaps flat against the wall. For a long moment, there's no change, no difference in the air pushing at me or the noise rattling my bones. And then I feel it. A slight reduction, getting larger. Slowly, the sound drops off to a weird juddering, and the blur of blades decelerates until I clearly see each rotation.

A few steps take me closer. So close I'm concerned I'll get my hair caught and die here, an idiot in a machine. I pull back slightly, shaking with eagerness. But it takes forever. I'm sure the soldiers must be running toward me right now, knowing someone has cut the power in here, where they have no business being. With the lights on, and nowhere to hide or run, I don't have a shot in hell.

The blades finally grind to a halt. Silence drapes the room, a heavy blanket. No time to be thankful for the absence of noise, though, and I screw up the last piece of courage I have left and duck under the thick slice of metal. The space is barely big enough for me, narrowing so quickly I have to crouch and wiggle my way past. It's dark at the back, and I'm shocked when my leading foot presses up against a hard surface. It's just the rim, I tell myself, feeling forward with one hand.

And then I touch the grille. A metal grille, covering my exit. A scream of frustration builds in my chest, and I slam my palm into the thin layer separating me from freedom. I hit it again, frustration and anger fueling my muscles. Nothing happens, and then behind me, in the room I am so desperate to escape from, I hear a noise. A creak. Voices.

"We've got Zaps on you. Come out with your hands up!" A woman's voice, stern and demanding. Professional.

I shove at the grate frantically, but the thin metal only gives slightly under my hands. Not enough. I squirm sideways, pressing my back against the sheet so I can push with my shoulders, bracing my hands against the inside of the blades. From here, I can only see a sliver of the room. I'm squashed into the four-foot-wide space holding the huge fan, my feet are wedged up against one of the blades, and I'm sandwiched between the grille and the huge machine. I press back, terrified, and at the same time full of sickening rage. Caught, I think. After everything I've achieved, caught. But I won't let them take me. I'd rather die.

The door, which had just been cracked wide enough for a voice before, opens far enough that I see the edge of it as it pushes into the room, and then the soldiers storm in. Four of them, their body armor a second skin made of black neoprene and Kevlar, and armed with Zaps that can deliver crippling blasts of energy straight into my flesh from however far they choose. I'm numb with terror, trying to press myself through the centimeter-wide holes perforating the grille behind me.

The soldiers walk toward my hiding place in the guts of the huge fan and get close enough for me to see their boots: heavy, rubberized material shining eerily clean. I can't see their weapons anymore, but they must have them pointed right at me. I cower, paralyzed.

Suddenly, one of them crouches and presses a gloved hand to the floor. I know those gloves—I've seen them on the Institute soldiers who sometimes march the streets. The material stops them from leaving psionic traces on everything they touch. Black, the same as the rest of their uniform, but with a circular space on the palms for skin contact, which makes for more efficient telepathy. I shiver, pressing back, my whole body crushed uncomfortably into the cold metal. They've brought a Reader with them. The woman rests on one knee and looks up.

Her gaze snaps onto mine when I'm hidden in the deep shadows of the fan box. She has me.

The moment spools out, my body frozen in fear. But she doesn't say anything, and her eyes... They're too human for someone hunting a kid. My mouth drops open as I recognize her. I recognize her.

"SAM, HEY KIDDO! Come lend us a hand?"

I look up, the sunlight, achingly bright, poured over everything. The grass in the city park is vivid and luxurious, and the burger in my hand drips thick grease into my palm, the same smeared over my chin from my feast. My dad is waving at me, standing by the grill with a woman I don't know. Stuffing the last morsel of rich meat and soft bread into my mouth, I jog over, wiping my palm on my trousers before remembering I'm supposed to look after them.

My dad merely smiles at me, indulgently. His son, at the company barbeque, for the first time ever. I grin back, happy to be there.

"Sam, this is Andrea. She's...uh...a friend from work." The woman is tall and dark-skinned, beautiful, with high cheekbones and cropped hair emphasizing her bone structure. She gives him a sort of sideways look that says thousands of things, and I stutter to a halt in front of them, holding my hand out. Friend, my ass. But my dad doesn't deserve to sit around missing my mom for the rest of his life.

"Nice to meet you!" I make sure to sound cheerful— welcoming—so she knows I'm okay with it. With them. She gives me a slow smile, blinking lazily in the hot light.

"You, too, Sam. I've heard a lot about you." Her eyes are kind.

HER EYES ARE still kind, but sharp, wary, and alert. A friend from work. If Andrea is a Reader—and, nuke, I had no idea from chatting to her on the grass at a perfectly normal barbeque—but if she's a Reader, and she's my dad's friend from work, then unmistakably, my dad is Institute. Not simply government, ignorant of the darker underbelly, but part of the organization hunting us. Hunting me. My bones melt in fear and pain. And then she speaks.

"He was here an hour ago."

What? She's lying. She saw me. I know she did. Which can only mean she's protecting me.

Then her voice rings out again, and I see her climb to her feet. "Well, he's either left, locked himself down, or run totally dry. Not a trace left of the brat. It'd take a stronger Reader than me to figure out what happened here. Maybe he used the door, ducked back inside. I doubt he could've gone through the fan! There's the grille blocking it for one, and the cameras and sensors outside the intake don't show anyone busting out. Move, search the corridors, surrounding area. He's not dangerous anymore—his powers are totally tapped, judging by the stamp on the floor here—but don't drop your guard."

"Well something blew out the med wing. He might have gotten hold of an EMP somehow. What about the fan stopping?" A gruff voice with attitude. I huddle against the grate, afraid they'll rethink the Reader's words and search anyhow. The grate bends in the middle, and I freeze, suddenly terrified I'll give myself away with a noise.

My dad's girlfriend hawks as if she's going to spit in disgust. "Must have been unrelated. Switch it back on, Grimes. The rest of you, move out."

I can't believe it, I'm safe. She's saved me. They're leaving! The relief is so strong I can barely hold my head up, my tense muscles turning to melted sugar. But I'm not alone yet. Finally, the door opens, someone grunts in effort, and then they're through, the door slamming behind them.

I go limp, my head thumping against the blade with a clang that would have gotten me dragged out by my bare feet if they'd still been in the room. The metal is cool and welcome after the heat of panic.

Until it starts to move, and suddenly I remember. "Switch it back on"—the words flood me with trepidation, and I realize the blade against my head is shifting. I jerk away in shock, and under my arm, another blade slowly pushes into me. Moving upward, dragging across my skin.

I fling myself backward against the grille again, twist myself around, and throw my full weight against it in total desperation. It gives a little, but the blade scrapes over my back, so slowly I can hardly bear it because I know any second now the force will increase. The speed will pick up, and I'll be sucked in and turned into Sam jam.

There's maybe a foot of space between the fan blade and the huge grate, not enough room to get any weight behind my shoves. I scream and curse under my breath, the noise sucked into the *whump whump* growing steadily louder.

Warming metal scrapes over my back, hits my elbow, scrapes over my shoulder, hits my elbow, again and again, bruising delicate flesh with repeated impact, no matter how slow it is. Soon it will be faster, my arm will break, get caught, and drag me in. I'll be mushed.

I yank my thoughts away, refusing to follow such a debilitating train of thinking, focusing on the vent covering. It's the only way out, and suddenly I'm pushing, shoving, growling, slamming myself into it with the greatest force I can muster. Again. Again. The fan behind me is a constant drag against my exposed back, and I shove weakly, beaten body aching, hopeless. It's hopeless.

I lean forward, resting my damp cheek against the cool surface of the thin yet insurmountable grate, and wait to die.

And wait. The fan gains momentum, spinning faster, pulling at me even though it's not hitting me anymore. I'm not even trying to escape, just pushed up against the grille in despair.

When the metal gives, it's such a surprise I nearly fling myself backward into certain death. The grille busts out of its frame, apparently unable to hold up to my full body weight after the blows to its center, and we slam to the ground, my fingers clawing at the punctured metal sheet in shock. The impact rattles my teeth, but hope rushes through me, powering my feet and wet-noodle muscles. I scramble up, running before I find my balance, careening off a shocked-looking lady, who is standing and staring.

The solar panels of the inner city uncomfortably hot on the sensitive skin on my feet, I lurch down the street, with no idea where I am or what I'm heading toward, powerless and weak.

But free.

# Serena

MY ASSESSMENT OF the situation proves accurate. When I push open the door to Ops, Abial is already leaning over a large comp table, scanning the reams of fast-moving text clearly comprising our mission briefing. Stupid speed-reader. That'll take me ages to read. My father is rapidly adding information to the display from his datapad, swiping new images and text files onto the table. He glances over, his curly, graying hair shadowing his permanently sad eyes. He looks exhausted, hollow cheeked, and wan. It's barely dawn now, and he's probably been up all night, putting together information we'll need, letting us get as much rest as possible. Maybe now I have a mission, he'll actually manage to talk to me.

"Agent Jacobs." The wry tone gives him away; he has decided to treat me like any other operative. Whether this is for my benefit or his doesn't matter.

"Sir." I'm pleased my voice is steady and strong, giving away none of my disquiet, and I march over to the huge tabletop screen to join in the briefing. We're being sent to Second City because a large group of Institute soldiers has recently left Fourth City on the tube, geared for military action. A group of Watch soldiers, ungifted military justice enforcers, appears to be preparing to join them.

The intelligence they've gathered leads the ARC techs to believe it's a manhunt; someone the Institute wants badly is on the loose in Second City. The soldiers from Fourth City are clearly going out to provide support for the local Institute and City Watch. And anyone the Institute wants so badly could also be useful to ARC. So ARC is sending in operatives of its own to find out what's going on, either back this person up or take them out, depending on what we find. To keep them from the Institute, either way.

Familiarizing myself with the layout of the City, memorizing the maps and going through the information available, doesn't fill me with confidence. There's not enough of it, not enough information, not enough knowledge. Not only are we gonna be out there by ourselves, against the full power of the local Institute plus extra squads, but worse, nobody really knows why. It's all loose guesswork from intercepted communication. If the Institute thinks it's worth putting in this much effort, ARC has to believe the same thing. At least that's the message I'm getting.

I keep my uneasiness from my face, knowing I have to accept my role as operative in the mission. If my father greeted me in any other way, I might have questioned him, but he's made it clear I'm a soldier and he is my leader. My superior, sending me on an unsupported, dangerous mission with a girl I don't trust. Urgh. I resist the urge to roll my eyes at him like Young Shannon would do.

Abial, meanwhile, is studiously avoiding my eyes as she sorts through equipment. I glance at the table, taking in the lack of weapons, and grimace. Getting through the Wall with weapons isn't too hard. A bribe here, an avoided scanner there. But getting onto the tube with anything dangerous would be suicide.

The tubes are the best-guarded places in the world because the governors are afraid of travel between the cities being cut off. Making the trip any way except the tube means leagues of slums, dead land, and inhospitable ground. It's slow, as well as dangerous and exposed. Kion was born in the deadlands and is one of the only people I know who travels to other cities overland, gone for months at a time, coming back weathered and thin. He doesn't talk about it much, but from the scraps I've heard, it doesn't sound like a good journey to make, even for a born nomad. I can't really blame the governors for not wanting to make the trip and building the tube in the first place. It's fast and relatively easy and good for most travel.

For ARC, it adds a whole mess of complications to a mission. So, no weapons, but we can lift some when we arrive. The tech will get through okay, as long as it looks like something civs would carry. I pick up one of the phony IdentCards and snicker. "Gabrielle Williams" is seventeen and a prospective university student. The photo they've used of me is unflattering, to say the least. I look like a serial killer.

Abial looks over at me and seems to want to ask what I find so funny, but clearly she thinks better of it. I sigh and flip the card toward her, using a wisp of power to guide it right to her hands. She looks surprised but takes it out of the air and smiles a little before wafting her own card over to me. The picture isn't much better. I smirk; maybe we've agreed to a truce, without saying a word. Maybe we both want to be professional. Maybe neither of us have forgiven the other, but now, in the light of an actual mission and the danger of death, we have to be on the same team.

My attention is drawn away as Kion's face fuzzes onto the screen; he's scruffy and worn-looking, as though he's been up all night too. He grins half-heartedly at us. "I wanted to say good luck, not that you need it. You're going to do great." He sounds a little scattered, as if he's concentrating on a dozen things at once. He probably is. But he's made the time to come around and wish us luck, and I grin back at him, reassured. His stoic presence has been a constant in my life for as long as I remember.

"Thanks, Kion. If you wanna give me a reason to make it back, move the C4 classes to next week. I've been looking forward to them for ages!"

He smirks, tucking his hair behind his ear. "Ah, maybe. Jue's pretty excited about them, though, so how about she catches you up?"

"You jerk!" I grin, forgetting for a moment that our commanding officer is there. My father clears his throat, though, and Kion colors ever so faintly, then nods to me and Abial, who is standing with an expressionless face.

"Take care. Remember your training." He cuts the communication before I have a chance to respond. I turn to shrug at Abial, wanting the comfort of our old camaraderie, hoping she's willing to set everything aside, for today at least. I start to smile but freeze when Abial yanks her card back, dropping mine on the table, and sending a thought right at me. *If you think we're friends again now, get your head out of your ass. You lied to me.*

The amount of hatred wrapped up in Abial's thoughtform makes me take a step backward. There's hidden currents under the message, a fathomless, stirring feeling I can't make out, a shadow in the deep waters of Abial's emotions. Is it repulsion? She never cared about any of the many queer people around at ARC. Is it different because it's about her? My ribcage throbs as though it's shrinking; I can't tell if I'm hurt or angry. I feel broken. Her face twists in a cruel sneer, and she shoulders her pack, long legs carrying her swiftly out of the room. I stare after her.

My father rests his hand on my shoulder and squeezes gently. When I look up, his eyes are kind, and I let myself lean against him for a moment. The desire to tell him what's going on—I fell for Abial and betrayed her trust completely—rises in me, but before I open my mouth, my father claps me on the shoulder and takes his hand away. "Whatever happened between you two is going to have to wait. I wouldn't send you with her if it wasn't the only choice. We've got a contact for you on the other side, one of Kion's boys. He's known the family forever, apparently. He says you can trust the guy. I wish the situation between you girls was different. But it's too risky to send either of you alone, and everyone else is compromised. We don't have long enough to take the dust roads through the dead land. Two young women aren't going to rouse much suspicion." He sighs deeply, rubbing the back of his neck. "If we could only get into their damned systems."

Pushing my hurt aside, I chew on my lip, nodding in agreement. If we could get into the Institute's systems, we wouldn't have to guess at the meaning of garbled communications. If we hacked the tube security, we could erase some of the data from the facial recog programs, and he could send Kion or another experienced operative. Instead, he's being forced to send his own daughter to a place where he won't be able to help me if things go wrong.

I shrug my shoulders, forcing lightness into my tone for his sake. "Eh, we'll be fine. We'll go, find out what they're up to, and sneak whatever or whoever they're after out from under them. I'll be back before you know it."


MY BRAVADO IS still in place twenty minutes later, when we head out of the hidden entrance to ARC, deep in the least-frequented area of the slums, far from the City Wall.

Dressed in a careful selection of browns and grays, we won't stand out from the workers. The sun is still low and gauzy in the red dust of the desert as we sneak through the sleeping townships. The broken buildings and rickety shacks are quiet, the population sleeping or out of sight. The oppressive heat outside always comes as a bit of a shock, even this early in the morning, and both of us are sporting attractive sweat stains by the time we reach the Wall. Still, it helps us look the part.

A tentative mental scan of the area and brief mind-to-mind conversation dealing only with the imminent and practical, and we agree there are no psionic Readers at the Wall. So we join the queue of ragged individuals heading through the Wall itself toward the factory district, or to clean the streets of the higher-class neighborhoods. I check my mental shields, nervous.

Entering the Wall is always a little awe-inspiring. Towering into the sky, the sparkling white monstrosity defies belief. There are no lines or marks to hint at the method of construction. It's an impossibility—proof of power beyond the understanding of most citizens. To me, it is the physical manifestation of the inequalities between the slums and the City itself, which is somehow always clean. The Wall is always sparkling, even on the slum side, where the sun bakes the ground and the dust blows freely. The guards are like the Wall: emotionless, efficient, and totally indifferent to what goes on around them.

My heart is in my throat as we approach those soldiers, and the barrier guarding the gaping maw of the main City entrance. It's if I've swallowed a rock. Keeping my nerves from my face takes all my attention, but zapping through takes only a few moments, and then we head into the City itself. I make sure I release my breath slowly as we join the queue of people going into the City to work, blending. Another normal day collecting credits, nothin' to see here, friends.

The stark differences between the City and the slums never fail to make my insides squirm. Outside, the population is huge-eyed and too thin. Children play in the dust and cough their lungs into bloody scraps as their parents try to eke out a living any way they can. The houses are built from recycled materials scrounged from the dumps.

But, oh, inside. Inside, the gleaming buildings are unnaturally clean and shiny. The main streets are shielded from the worst of the sun's rays by clever interlocking transparent sheets, protecting the delicate skin of the rich. The superstructures are huge, beautiful, flowing edifices creating abstract shadows on the solar-paneled roads. Apartments meld seamlessly in rolling curves; gleaming silver and reflective, the skin of a huge dragon. It's no wonder people long to be invited into this clean and wholesome world. I'd stay if I didn't know better.

Abial nudges me gently in the side, indicating I should stop gawping, and we turn into a side street, walking as if we belong here. Our clothes are new enough that nobody blinks an eye when we detach from the trudging line of downtrodden and slip out one of the separate barrier exits for citizens, instead of remaining and being sorted onto a shuttle for work. Hopefully, right now, we look like two teenagers coming in for training. *Honest, buddy, I just wanna be part of the Watch when I grow up, so I can meet Gav Belias and have his beautiful, dimpled babies.*

We duck out of view into a preselected garden square, the sheer waste of which almost makes me swear out loud. The fresh water used to keep this nook green and fresh could have grown food for several families. We quickly tidy our clothing, clip our hair into the latest City fashion, and clean our shoes on the thick grass. Our leggings need a good slapping to remove the dust of the townships, but a little bit of Talent takes care of it quietly. We scan each other for any tiny clue that might give us away, in the same way all trainees have practiced a thousand times, and nod confirmation at each other, satisfied.

"Ready?" I form the word carefully, letting the soft vowels of an educated citizen change my pronunciation from my normal, rough accent. Elocution lessons are the worst, but now I'm out on a mission and need to soften my coarse speech, I'm glad I had them.

Abial smirks, her toffee-colored hair neat and her fighter's calluses hidden by a pair of soft faux-leather gloves. She's so beautiful in the full light I have to force myself to drag my gaze over her professionally instead of in admiration. "Certainly. We'd best get to the station." The cultured voice sounds strange and at odds with Abial's flint-hard eyes and the musculature visible in her folded arms. She needs to adjust her posture or she'll get us both caught.

*Stand less like a soldier.* I send her a wisp of power, with an image of her tensed body poised on the balls of her feet. I also force my own muscles to relax, sinking into the persona I have to embody if we want to make it through the security checks at the tube. I smile, an open smile, the smile of someone with few cares in the world, and offer the crook of my arm to my companion. Abial returns the smile, and we spin on our slippered heels, leaving our rough selves and the small green garden behind us.

As we walk, we chatter about nonsense, making lighthearted conversation. No one even spares us a glance, except for a few young men we pass, some of whom offer frank but unthreatening grins. Life really is different inside.

Outside, those grins would be violence-promising leers, and two girls wouldn't be walking alone. Well, the two of us do have a few advantages the average slum-dweller doesn't, but still. Here, the doorways are empty, no sneering prostitutes giving us the once-over and no cripples crouching with hands outstretched, braving the sun's rays to beg, knowing their lives are almost finished anyway, starvation or cancer a constant threat. There aren't any bundles of rags marking slumped bodies that may or may not already be corpses.

The citizens walk the streets, totally confident in their own safety. And we appear to be exactly like them; nothing out of the ordinary, except our eyes are scanning for threats and camera lenses. We spot members of the Watch walking the streets with negligent ease, and evade them effortlessly. It's almost insulting how simple it is to walk around the City. It's as though my years of training are being wasted on these fools.

There's a hum in the air around the tube station when we get there. New arrivals hurry out of the imposing square building, a fat, squatting toad at the end of the shining street. Family members exclaim with delight and greet their loved ones. Off-duty soldiers slap hands on the backs of their crew as they return from what must be out-of-City assignments.

The queue to enter the building stretches for four blocks, with people waiting contentedly in the shade, and no sense of irritation or urgency. Vendors, slum dwellers, who hope to earn enough credits to buy citizenship for themselves and their families, walk the sidewalks with trays of food and drink for the citizens' convenience. The air virtually vibrates with the happiness of people who know those in charge are working in their best interest and are looking after them.

I spot a dwell—slum dweller—I know, and quickly twist so my back is facing the man who sells trinkets to the kids at ARC every Sevenday. There are any number of ways to be caught in the City, and being recognized is just one of them. There's no reason he would know my cover identity, and it's hard for people who aren't trained to keep their microexpressions under control. I need to be more careful.

We join the line, trying to look as though we belong and fill the time talking about the wonderful sights we've seen and how exciting the University courses seem. How thrilled "Gabrielle's" father will be that I want to follow in his footsteps and study at Memphiste University, home of the greatest scientists for generations.

The line shuffles forward, a few older couples sparing us looks of condescending affection, patronizing "Isn't it wonderful to be young and have your whole life ahead of you?" sort of looks. A strapping lad in his twenties spits into a handkerchief and then drops it with a look of disdain, throwing the rest of his food pack after it. I watch him waste the food, wanting to throw him over the Wall to see the six-year-olds combing through sewage, looking for items they can sell so they can afford a few scraps of bread. But obviously telekinetically chucking someone up in the air would blow my cover. So the food pack lies in the filtered sunlight until a bony woman—clearly a dwell lucky enough to get a chit to work the streets today—picks it up. She disappears down a side street with it clutched in her thin hands, as though someone is going to take it away from her.

The ire must have been rising in my eyes, because Abial nudges me with a sharp elbow, harder than necessary, and giggles, gesturing surreptitiously at a young soldier. I swallow my anger and join Abial in watching the handsome, dark-haired man marching into the military entrance. His uniform does nothing to detract from the gentle beauty of his face, golden-brown skin, or his flashing dark eyes. He spares a lopsided smile for us before disappearing through the large black door, and I glance at Abial, grinning in turn at the light blush visible on her tan skin. "Ooh, you're so handsome, mister. Will you take me to the school dance?" I tease quietly.

Abial abruptly whirls toward me, eyes full of rage. "You...you shut up, Ser—" There is a hint of Talent in her command, but nothing I can't resist with my own power, in time to stop her from getting the whole name out. It could cause further trouble for us down the line; the Institute might end up tagging us facially, and if they get my name as well, it might come back to bite me if the wrong person gets read.

"No need to call me 'sir,' Laura. I'm not that butch!" The emphasis on the false name cuts through whatever caused the flare of temper, and Abial nods, the color in her cheeks fading. A quick glance around convinces me nobody has noticed anything amiss; just two friends teasing each other as they wait. Sour thoughts about our dead friendship lodge in my temples, giving me a headache.

The rest of our queuing is done in tense, awkward silence, doing absolutely nothing for my growing nerves. Abial is acting totally out of character and putting us both in danger; another unpredictable outburst could cost us our lives or, if the Institute gets ahold of us, our minds. We shuffle through the wide doorway and hold our IdentCards over the reader, while a scanner passes over our bodies in a visible blue line. My heart stutters as it turns orange on my bag, but Abial is totally unruffled, and I follow her, grateful for her confidence, as she marches down the arrow flashing on the floor to a bag-check area.

My mind is racing, wondering what could be in my bag. Surely the techs at ARC checked it before they left? Did they miss something? Maybe I should have gone through it myself, but we were in such a rush. Now I wish I'd taken the time. If whatever's in the bag gets us caught... I stuff my hand in my pocket and hope no one notices my clenched fist. When we stop, a brusque soldier, who resembles a brown and pockmarked potato, pats the table in front of him with a fleshy hand. "Bags here, IdentCards to me." His tone is professional, and he doesn't seem alarmed.

"Yes, officer." Abial sounds perfect, and she rolls her eyes at me, feigning disinterest at the holdup. She doesn't look even slightly nervous.

Forcing myself to remain calm as well, we plop our bags where he indicated and hand over our ICs. My heart pounding, we wait as the cards are scanned. He places them on an electronically marked grid to the side of the table, then rummages through our possessions with alacrity. I keep my face an affected mask of boredom, like this happens every day. As if I know what will happen next. It's a good thing they don't have a bioscan on me; I'm sure my racing pulse would be flagged as a suspicious reaction. He hauls out a datapad and turns it around, so it's facing me. It should be one of the special ones ARC keeps for undercover work, but what if somehow it's not? What if someone made a mistake? Usually we'd have gone through everything ourselves, but there wasn't any time! My stomach turns, but I reach for it anyway.

"Turn this on, please," he says sharply. My eyes slide sideways, subtly scoping out the immediate area, in case the mission is blown and we have to fight our way out. To the right of us, a middle-aged couple is having their own belongings investigated. They don't look suspicious at first glance, but neither should we. I hope against hope this is a random screening, and we haven't already messed up, and manually switch on the machine. Holding my breath, I enter my password when I'm prompted. An innocent display comes up, and I breathe a sigh of relief, but as unobtrusively as possible, try to keep it off my face. The soldier clicks into a few files, then holds a hand-scanning unit over the device and grunts when it beeps.

"Thank you, have a pleasant trip." He dismisses us, sliding our cards back over the table, and that's the end of it. We're free to go. My fingertips tingle as I pick my card up, and I hastily shove my things back into my bag.

"Have a good day!" My bright tone causes potato face to give us a bemused look, and we quickly slip back through the crowd to join the line of people heading to Second City. The queue moves fast now, and I note eighteen cameras and twelve scanning units which must have clocked us. If this mission goes south, our faces will be registered as threats, and I'll never come here again. I look around, trying to put the thought from my mind. The station itself isn't especially beautiful, but the squeaky-clean nature and organized chaos are interesting. I don't think I've ever seen this many people in one place, yet everything is still fairly quiet. A low hum of conversation fills the air, punctuated by beeping sounds from various pieces of technology. And that's it. Soon we find ourselves at the exit.

We climb a steep flight of stairs and head out onto the platform, where gray concrete stretches several hundred meters in each direction. The tube, it seems, is aptly named. I feel as if I'm in a giant display unit. I've seen the tube from outside, but this is ridiculous. In front of me is the Wall. A dozen meters above my head is the transparent aluminum shield protecting the City's open spaces from the sun.

The tube punches a hole in the Wall and then curves out toward the mountains, which I can barely make out, hazy in the distance. A glowing barrier sits around the tracks, divided into hexagons, delineated by flashing strips of faux-lightning. Anything thrown or shot at the tube will be instantly vaporized when it makes contact with the barrier. It keeps the tube safe, but I shudder, remembering the blackened ruin of my friend Tian's wrist.

Chased by Institute soldiers, she'd stumbled against the barrier and lost her whole hand. Somehow she'd managed to get away and make it to a safe house, permanently crippled, but at least she was still alive, and out of the Institute's clutches. Psionic power has no effect on the barrier itself. You have to take out the source projecting it outward so Tian couldn't catch herself. I'm in as much danger as a normal person from the barrier. It isn't a sensation I'm used to. I shiver in a sudden wash of air and realize the train is coming.

The platform doesn't even shake when the huge vehicle shoots out of the Wall like a bullet from a gun and stops smoothly in front of us, the cone-shaped nose disappearing into a dark hole past the steps we used. I resist the urge to fidget impatiently as the passengers from Second City alight on the other side of the platform, and then the doors in front of us whoosh open in a gust of warmth. People get on in an orderly fashion.

We obediently wait our turn and then step aboard. I stifle a snort; it's so much neater than anything outside. The inside of the carriage, however, is nothing special, plastic seats arranged in twos, and bag storage. Every table is a datapad charge surface. Not cheap. Citizens can't be expected to travel without a fully charged computer; that would be shocking! Google forbid they have to detach from the net for as much as a second! They might miss an important message. I swing my bag onto the storage rack and take a seat, short legs fitting easily under the table. Abial has a bit more trouble and swears under her breath as she bangs her knee.

I cock an eyebrow at her warningly. Polite citizens don't swear, and if they do, they definitely don't use the expletive Abial did. Fortunately, she said it quietly, and no one is paying any particular attention to us. People are settling in, getting out their datapads and snacks. Some of them are already pressing their fingers and thumbs against each other in precise combinations. They're obviously unwilling to take even a moment away from whatever they're doing. I settle in as well. It's important we look as though we're used to this, rather than drawing attention to ourselves.

The mission briefing prepared us for getting through security and onto the tube but hadn't told us what to do after. This part is up to us. As the train pulls out of the station, the landscape zooming past at frightening speed, I paste a disinterested look on my face and gaze out the window, instead of looking around eagerly like I wish I could. Abial sets up her datapad and starts typing. Hopefully we look like nothing more than bored students.

Once we get to the other station, it's only one more set of security, and then we'll meet Kion's contact. If we're lucky, he'll have figured out a place for us to hole up; reconnaissance is definitely needed before we jump in. Powerful as we both are, there's no way the two of us can take on a squad of Institute soldiers on our own; we'd get beaten to paste. We need to figure out what's happening and come up with a plan to counter the Institute. There's a lot of equipment that would make our jobs easier, as well, and if Kion's guy can't get it, we're gonna have to rob a Watch station first. I frown a little. We've done mock exercises for hitting up a Watch station. Watch soldiers aren't gifted; that's reserved for the special forces of the Institute. But they're still well trained and armed. It won't be easy if we have to do it. Still, there's nothing to gain from going back over the four methods I know for a station hit until I check out the situation in Second City. For now, I need to blend in and pass the time. We're not safe here; we can't talk.

I glance around the cabin slowly, keeping the bored expression on my face. Two tables over, a unit of soldiers in tall boots and well-fitted uniforms decorated with badges and ribbons are playing a card game.

There are eight of them, and I make a game of secretly observing them in the reflection from the window. They're all young, fit, and strong: five men and three women, all sturdy and athletic-looking. I'm counting their Zaps when I realize I'm being watched. The handsome soldier from the queue smirks at me with a dangerous dimple and blows me a kiss. I frown and nearly turn away, when suddenly his face clicks into place, and I realize who it is. Gav Belias himself! My mouth slackens slightly in shock, as his friends smirk and jostle him. Obviously they think I'm checking them out in a girly way, not a soldiery way. Good. They won't see me as a threat if they think I'm interested in him romantically.

How arrogant, to assume I'm looking at him for any reason except to assess a threat. He's pretty, but not that pretty. The dark-skinned woman to his right with the gold beads in her hair is much more my type. The thought brings a moment of hollow amusement. Great, now I can't even make gay jokes in my own head without thinking about Abial's anger. I arrange my face back into a look of boredom, raise an eyebrow at Gav Belias, and return my attention to the fascinating view rushing past. Jue is gonna wet herself when she finds out I was on the same train as him. I have to force myself to focus on the outside world instead of glancing back to his reflection in the glass. Unimpressed as I'd love to be, he's still a bona fide celebrity, and I resent how tempted I am to look again, just for a moment.

Resolutely, I peer through the transparent aluminum. The tube is suspended over the townships now. Peasant children have clambered up the supports and are gawping at the vehicle as it streams past, though they can't get too close, because of the vaporizing barrier. The barrier is an endless source of entertainment for the kids, who love to throw things at it and dare each other to get close, but its real purpose is beyond their understanding. The tube is the artery of the government. Sever it and cities would be alone, cut off. And with no imports and exports going in and out, life would change dramatically. Google knows how long it took to erect, but the entire country would be lost without it.

No wonder they protected it the way they did. And protect it they must. If the slum dwellers aren't kept passive by the Institute—pushed down mentally, with any resistance crushed—they would try to overpower the Watch and sever the tube in order to cut off military backup arriving from the other Cities. This is only one of the reasons any hint of rebellion is terminated immediately, with extreme prejudice. And that's why ARC exists.

As I watch, we pass over the edge of the townships, the shacks here not even close to being buildings; just shelters built with whatever people find. Broken pieces of transal lean against walls made from food packaging and ancient metal poles. This is all the people have available to them, dug from dumps and scrounged from the City's trash heaps. All the government will let them have, and the Institute finds anyone who thinks they are entitled to more. Finds them, and removes them from the equation.

Soon, we're speeding up, and I can hardly make out the different shanties anymore. It's a blur as we head for the mountains. The land beyond the slums turns swiftly to desert; aching miles of arid land, stretching as far as the eye can follow. It gives me a headache, so I close my eyes, pretending to sleep, but really daydreaming about a successful mission.

If I fail, there's the ever-present risk of death or capture. But what preys on my mind most is the idea of messing this mission up. If I do, there's no way my father will let me go after Damon. And if I can't go after Damon, I don't know if anyone ever will.

After he was taken in an attack that took out half our people, my father made the decision. We didn't have the people power to try to go after him. There wasn't enough of us. And later, when we found a safe space to hide in, there was so much to rebuild and reestablish. Two teams went after Damon, spent weeks tracking him, but turned up nothing. The Institute hide too well. I'll never forget the look on my father's face when he told me we had to stop burning resources looking for my brother. I know he thought he couldn't put one boy's life against our entire group. But I never forgave him, not really. That wedge still colors our entire relationship.

When the transport slows, I open my eyes and glance at the digital timepiece on the wall. Barely an hour has passed; Google, this was a fast journey. People start scuffling, standing, and grabbing their bags. The soldiers are already up and waiting by the door. Abial shuts off her datapad and grins at me. "All right, Gabrielle, let's go meet our ride."

"Sure thing, Laura. We're supposed to go to the East exit, I think." As we wait in line to disembark, I deliberately keep my gaze away from the soldiers, busying myself with the datapad balanced in my hand. I don't want them to pay too much attention to me, just in case we come across each other again.

It's obvious these troops are being sent over to back up the local Watch presence; Gav Belias isn't only renowned for his good looks—he's also a talented tactician and brilliant fighter—according to the ARC files on him. He'll be wanted wherever the action is. I'll have to look his files up again to make sure I'm prepared if I have to fight him, but for now, I want him to remember me as nothing more than a star-struck girl. If he's as good as they say he is, he won't be easily fooled, and many things could give me or Abial away as more than we appear. Fortunately, there are several people between us, and he's not paying much attention to me. For now, it seems, we're safe.

# Part Four

# Sam

KNOWING THERE ARE cameras everywhere on the street, I detour into an apartment building. A man pushing a pram of screaming toddlers is so distracted by the children he actually thanks me—a kid in an obviously not-for-outside smock—as I hold the door.

I need to find clothes and food. If I get some energy back, I can loop the camera feeds around me, to repeat a little of the past video, instead of showing my path. But first I need shoes. My bare feet are leaving traces I can't avoid. Until I get shoes, I may as well be painting huge arrows on the ground saying "Escaped prisoner!"

And they'll be after me, full force. I broke out of their secure area in a way they clearly didn't know enough to expect. They'll want me. Badly.

I trudge across the open lobby of the huge building, the air conditioning chilling me to the bone. Fortunately, it's nighttime, possibly late, so there aren't a lot of people about, and I hustle around the corner unmolested, skipping the elevators. The Institute will be here in minutes, maybe less, so going up might buy me a little time, but will also trap me. I stumble down the corridor instead. I don't have a plan, and I must look as bad as I feel because a woman letting herself out of apartment 106 catches my eye and lets out a little squeak of surprise and horror.

I step toward her, trying to look threatening. Fear is a much faster reaction than sympathy, and there isn't time to convince her to help me of her own accord. As much as I hate doing it, intimidation is my only shot at getting into her apartment, where I can find the things I need.

"Let me in, and I won't hurt you." Hopefully the mere fact I'm male and scruffy and probably quite mad-looking in my hospital-style gown, will be enough to override the skinny fourteen-year-old geek part. Her eyes flick from side to side, and I lift my arm, making a fist and hating myself for the fear I see in her face. I'm sorry.

When she still doesn't move, I shove past her. The kitchen is right off the front door, and I make a beeline for the fridge, where I find a bag of milk in the door. I grab it and gulp the whole thing greedily, the coolness spreading in my stomach. It cramps in protest, but I ignore it. I need sustenance, now. I don't know how long they had me for, but I know from experience the only way to get my power back up and running is food and sleep.

Sleep isn't an option, so hopefully, I can get enough food to give me the energy I desperately need. Behind me, the front door snicks closed, and I glance sideways, but the woman's gone. She'll call the Watch, no doubt about it. I would if someone barged into my house resembling a hospital escapee. They'll be here any second, and I'm leaving traces all over everything I touch.

But without food I'm dead.

A rummage in the first cupboard delivers a jar of peanut butter, and though unscrewing the lid takes a good second longer than I'd prefer, the rich, creamy paste is worth it. I actually feel the protein pouring energy into my leaden limbs as I suck it down. Then, abandoning the kitchen, I manage a weak jog to the hall cupboard and grab the first dark-colored, hooded jacket I find. I shove my bare feet into a large pair of boots. Good enough. Time to go; I have the absolute necessities. I cram the jar into my new pocket and bolt for the sliding glass doors leading onto a small balcony. The railing is waist high and I brace my hands on it, managing to clamber over even in my weakened state. When I hit the ground on the other side, I stagger off.

Sirens squeal down the road in front of the apartment building right as I sneak out the gate in back.

Thirty seconds later, a Watch patrol appears at the end of the alleyway I'm in, and I duck into an adjoining street as fast as I can. I'm not totally sure where I am, but the milk and peanut butter are hitting my bloodstream, energizing me. The food, along with the terror spiking my body with adrenaline, is enough to rouse my deadened power into a pale imitation of its usual robustness. It's enough. I flick it out, jumping onto the data streams buzzing in the air around me, and am able to pull up a map of the area in my mind. I immediately use the Watch's patrol frequencies to mark their locations so I can stay clear of them, then make sure no cameras are picking me up.

Once I'm sure they aren't, I head for the north edge of the factory district, wanting to put distance between myself and the people hunting me. Get back to familiar territory. Not too familiar, though—they'll have been all over my house and school hours ago. I can't ever go back there. But I need to find somewhere to rest and recover—stay ahead of them, and find out where they're keeping my mother.

I grit my teeth and tense my feet to stop the boots slipping off as I gracelessly half jog through the heavy night.

The strip lights lining the edges of the buildings illuminate everything on the main streets, so I avoid them, sticking to smaller roads that don't have solar paneling. I've used the panels to track people in the past, so I assume the Institute has figured that out. Gait is pretty distinctive, after all—you can disguise almost anything except the way you walk—so if I step on the electronic panels, I'll have to use my power to mess up the traces I leave. And I'm too weak right now. So I avoid them and stay tuned in to the data streams, as best I can, to keep abreast of the people hunting me.

But my concentration is shot, so my power is thready and unreliable. My heart is pounding hard, my throat dry and full of phlegm rattling uncomfortably as I pant. I narrowly avoid getting sandwiched between two patrols approaching from different directions and end up stumbling down a roughly coated road, boots catching and tripping me slightly with every step.

Finally, I grind to a halt outside a building I recognize, bending over to rest my hands on my knees for a moment as my lungs clamor for air. When I'm somewhat recovered, I stagger to the side of the street and lean my shoulder against a smooth window. I want to press my face and hands against its coolness, but it would leave traces. I'm pasting psychic residue to the surface, even through my new hoodie, but unless they track me here and place their hands in this specific place, it should be okay. I hope. I'm not super clear on how Readers' powers work, but I know bare skin leaves the most behind, skin oils and particles all carrying little scraps of information about their previous owner.

Anyway, it's the window or the ground while I figure out my next move. My legs are shaking so hard I don't trust them to hold my weight now momentum isn't keeping me moving forward. Resting is good—amazingly good—but I know I have to decide on a direction and press on.

I look left and see that I'm outside a textile factory I often walk past to get to the water distribution point. It's fourteen stories, with a huge window at the front I know leads into a room displaying massive wheels of brightly

colored thread. It's as good a place as any to lay low for a
little while. Not for long. They'll track me, no doubt about it.
A low-level Reader wouldn't find me, but I know enough of
the Institute to know they'll bring in the big guns, get their
best trackers after me, even if it's just to find out how I
nulled the chips they slotted into my brainpan.

Sniffing, I swallow the resulting mucus—spitting would
leave a physical marker with vestiges of my thoughts and let
them get a glimpse at my inner self—and lurch to the door.
It's a big steel affair, bashed and dented with decades of use.
The electronic lock is the kind that reads the chip in the
thumb and scans a database of registered users, so it takes
me longer than it usually would to find someone to
impersonate.

While I work, my spine itches with anticipation of
thundering boots running after me, Zaps swinging up to
splatter me against the metal. I wonder if they'll shoot to kill,
or only to maim. Not that it matters. I'm dead either way.

Finally, it clicks open, and I trip, my feet catching on the
lip of the threshold, almost sending me headlong into the
building. I really need to rest—I'm useless and dazed. If the
cameras weren't all on the same system, I wouldn't even
have been able to loop them long enough to make it here. I
can't risk moving again until I've recovered more of my
power.

Staggering forward, I look around. The room is one of
those low-ceilinged affairs making me feel the weight of the
whole building creaking and heaving above me. A red LED
display lets me know it's a little after three in the morning.
Maybe two hours before the next office shift comes in.
Machines thrum, power palpable in the air, but there
probably aren't many people around at this time. I hope.

I thud into a few filing cabinets on my way to the desk, bruising my hipbone, and snarl. I'm beaten up enough, thanks. I groan with relief as I collapse into a chair and yank open the desk drawers. Never mind I'm imprinting my presence all over everything, the oils from my fingertips leaving little Sam stamps—traces of my thoughts and feelings for them to investigate. I need supplies. More food, if possible, but most importantly, tech. I need technology I can take with me. Without it, I'm just a kid stumbling away from an army, blind and useless. With a computer, I might have a chance.

The first three drawers only yield office equipment—sheets of fiberpaper, staples, a few cases of data chips, digital pens, etc. The next one I try is locked with an old-fashioned padlock. Nuke, I swear, pushing back a little in my chair and giving it the evil eye. If it's locked, it stands to reason there's something useful in there. Somebody's data pad, maybe. I'd take a comm unit about now. But I'm not going to be able to get it open. Not without bolt cutters or some serious crowbar action, and I'm probably too weak to use any kind of physical tool, anyway. It's a little ironic—this archaic device would be useless against a telekinetic, but I, who can hack into banks from my bathroom if I so desire, am totally stumped.

Upset and frustrated, I kick the cabinet, making an echoing boom that scares me. If there are still workers on the floor, they might have heard. I reach out, sweaty fingers slipping on the metal, and try to force the drawer, hoping against hope I'll be able to pop the thing open. But it barely even creaks.

Deciding I've pushed my luck enough, I spin in the chair, turning to face the ancient computer squatting on the table. I boot it up and use it to get a quick look at the blueprints of the factory, then check in on the Institute soldiers trailing me. The Watch is buzzing all over the area, where I bolted from the apartment, and it looks as if they have a team on my trail. At least I assume that's what the slow-moving broadcast of uninterpretable data signals turning into the alleyway I ran down is.

I stand up and head for the back door, leading onto the factory floor. Now I know where they are, I think I can take the chance to sleep. I need my powers to stand even a sliver of a shot at avoiding them, and the food only helped a bit. They're behind me, following air traces now I have shoes on, and I should have a couple of hours. If not, I'm screwed, and at least this way I'll get some sleep.

As stealthily as I can, I nip down the corridor, then take the stairs to the roof. The blueprint indicated there was a water tank and machinery up there. Maybe I can find a place to hunker down, out of sight of any helichoppers in the area. When I finally reach the small door leading out to the roof, I pull my sleeve over my hand before I open it. The hinges creak and protest as I shove and slide through the gap. The open space greeting me is wide and long, plastic tiling with metal I-beams holding them in place. I stick to the struts in the hope the iron will help hide my passing, feeling horribly exposed, even on the edge, and head for the water tank. It will give me shelter, I hope. A safe place.

The roof creaks under my feet as I hurry across, but it only takes a moment or two of exposure before I reach the huge, squat cylinder. Then, with a last glance around, I drop to my knees and curl up under a large pipe, praying really hard I won't sleep for too long. I know I won't be able to keep ahead of the soldiers if I don't rest, though; my head is pounding and my limbs are shaky with exhaustion and stress.

I need the sleep, or I'm not going to make it.

I DON'T KNOW how much time passes before the *whump whump* of a chopper passing overhead jerks me from my slumber. I bash my shoulder as I jolt upright in shock and curse as the day's events catch up with me, then crouch in the shadow of the huge metal pipe and make myself as small as possible. It's still dark, so it's probably not quite morning.

The chopper banks and flies off over the buildings. Either I got lucky or it's calling in reinforcements. Probably reinforcements. They wouldn't have a Reader in the air—they need direct contact with my path or things I've touched to hunt. So if the chopper saw me, it will be calling someone to come in and help from below.

Whichever way, it's time to go, and at least I feel stronger as I get up and jog toward the edge of the building, heading for the handrail marking an emergency exit. Cautiously, I poke my head out, then immediately fling myself backward in shock. There's an elec-car parked below, and something in me recognizes it as an Institute vehicle.

My heart pounds in my chest, and my palms slick with sweat. Are they inside already? Looking for signs of my passing? I touched a bunch of stuff in there—my traces must be all over. I creep back to the edge and peek as carefully as I can. A Watch vehicle is also parked two blocks over, although I can only see one soldier, of indeterminate gender, scuffing their feet as they walk into a construction yard across the way.

Only one car? So not a full alert, but it could easily turn into one. Maybe they're still scoping out a bunch of different possibilities...but it will only take a Reader going into the front room for a moment to lead to dozens of vehicles and soldiers descending on me.

I dither, torn between hiding and hoping they move on, then making a run for it, when a creak from behind makes the decision for me. It must be the door to the building opening. I'm shielded by the tank, but only for moments; once they're on the roof, they'll be able to see me. I hurl myself over the edge in such haste I miss my footing on the rung of the ladder against the side of the building and clang painfully against the metal, feet scrambling for grip. As soon as I have purchase, I scuttle down, convinced a Reader is hot on my trail—or will be soon. I look at my feet as I climb, in the hopes I'll go faster, but the back of my neck tingles with anticipation of a Zap shot and an energy burst that will fling me off the ladder and onto the hard surface of the sidewalk below.

Nothing comes, and a moment later, I hit the ground running, sprinting down the street as fast as I can, not caring if I draw attention to myself. As I pass the Institute car, I slow for a second to screw with the engine, dragging my hand across the hood and messing with the electronics inside so it won't even start. A bunched-up black object in the back of the car catches my attention as I do so, and I grind to a halt. A bag. They'll have to follow me on foot, now, and that gives me a better chance. But I could still use whatever I can get my hands on.

It takes a second. I can't afford to click the lock and grab the bag, but the thought of what might be in there is worth it. Gear. Water. I have nothing, and I'm running blind.

A yell breaks the silence behind me, and a burst of energy fired from a Zap slams into the side of the car right as I snatch my hand clear. The metal sheet caves in, punched by an invisible giant, and I backpedal, flinging myself away and around the other side of the vehicle. Body shaking, I press against it, panting, mind skittering as I frantically try to make a decision.

I can't fight them, but taking the guns out would be a good start. Power fizzing inside me for the first time in too long, I reach for the Zaps with my mind, looking for the specific electronic wiring that passes power from the battery pack to the barrel. And then I open the connection as far as it goes, wider than it's supposed to be set unless you're planning to destroy a building.

Then I connect the firing mechanism. The recoil of the gun going off might even break his hand if I'm lucky.

There's a blast so loud my ears ring, and behind, I faintly make out the sound of screaming. It worked! But all the noise has drawn the attention of the Watch guy, and he's running toward me, shouting into his comm, Zap raised. I drag my Talent out of the first guy's Zap—he's dropped it on the roof in shock—and throw it out, an invisible attack on the machinery the Watchman carries. My power races through the connections and down the wiring. Just in time, because I see his finger tighten on the trigger, in slow-mo. But the gun is useless, blocked by my power.

He's only about twenty yards away, though, and will be on me in seconds, so I hurl myself upward, diving into the car. I have a new array of scrapes and bruises, but I'm in the driver's seat and pressing my hands against the dash, undoing the damage I wrought and reopening connections. The car starts without me needing to do anything except this—hands pressed in direct communication with its innermost workings. The engine whines as the car bursts forward, slamming me back against the seat.

I glance up to see the soldier sprinting toward me, in the rearview mirror, and in my terror, forget I have to steer. The car smashes onto the sidewalk, tilting wildly, and my stomach lurches as two wheels leave the ground for a moment, then crash back onto the road with a violent jolt.

After a heart-stopping bounce, it steadies, leaving me clutching the steering wheel and shooting down the street, the impotent soldier yelling and cursing in my wake as he tries and fails to catch up.

Sick with fear and waves of adrenaline, I spin the car onto the first street I can, and again, not knowing where I'm heading. Just away. Outside the window, I recognize my neighborhood but know it's not safe here.

With a one-handed death grip on the wheel, I press my other palm to the GPS, programming a course in. For a moment, I do nothing except lean back, breathing heavily and trying not to be sick, and then I screw my courage up as tight as it will go. I scream a sort of mad war cry as I let go of the wheel completely, grab the door handle, yank it open, and throw myself out. My shoulder crashes painfully into the hard road, followed by the rest of my body in a heavy rush.

When I stagger to my feet, I see the car continuing happily on its course, with one door flapping open. I hope it doesn't hit any pedestrians, and then hope further that the Institute will follow their vehicle and miss the fact that I'm no longer in it. At least for a while.

Buoyed up by my success, I sling the bag I stole over my shoulder and sprint off down the road. The sky is lightening to a misty gray above me, and I have to get off the streets. They'll track the vehicle easily, figure out I'm not with it, and retrace its path. From here on out I need to be unpredictable enough to confuse them. Keeping this in mind, I head back toward the richer part of town, hood pulled up to hide my face, still looping the camera feeds as I pass.

# Serena

THERE'S A MAJOR military presence in the Second City station, but citizens from the tube are rushed through a body scanner no one is really paying attention to and released toward their pickup points. It's all too obvious the soldiers are worried about someone leaving, not someone arriving. Super. That bodes well for our exit. Our leaving strategy is flimsy at best, and clearly getting through security in the other direction will be nigh impossible if it remains this tight.

Not knowing what or who the Institute is reacting to, we've been incapable of making a solid plan of any kind, let alone coming up with specific exit strategies. We don't even know what we're hunting, yet. If it's an item that won't make it through the scanners, we could drop it off with Kion's mystery friend. If it's a person, well, it depends if we get to them in time.

The chances of us pulling off a two-man rescue effort aren't high. But you learn to be adaptable at ARC, and if we need to put together a plan on the fly, that's what we'll do. Worst case scenario: the mission goes south and we can't get back on the tube. Then we'd have to shack up in the townships here for a while, try to lie low until the dust clears, and figure out an extraction. Assuming we're not dead, of course. There's no way we can take on the Institute by ourselves, so if we're beaten to the target, the mission is over. The best we could hope for then would be information to take back to ARC.

"Laura, Gabrielle? Welcome to Second City." The voice greeting us is polite and soft. It takes a split second for my brain to process, and then I turn and smile what I hope is a winning smile.

"Oh, yes. Hello. Are you our escort?" Abial's voice is soft and simpering. Gross, but effective at blending us in.

The boy who spoke appears to be around fifteen and is impeccably dressed in City fashion—a sharply cut gray suit, silver collar tips and an expensive comm unit riding the curve of his upper ear. His features are interesting. Traces of what could be Korean heritage are evident in the darkness and angles of his eyes. He tilts his head and speaks into the comm, the throat mic stuck to his neck flashing green. As he does so, he makes an *A* with his fingers, so nonchalantly it appears he's merely twisting his hands in boredom as he chats over the comm. The *A* sign—the signal we were told to look for. But the boy has recognized us easily. Do we stand out that much? Had he been told ahead of time who we are and what we look like? Or have we already given ourselves away? "Yes, Tomas, I have them. We'll be around in a minute."

We blink at each other for a moment, confused, and then the boy gestures grandiosely toward the street corner, his dark eyes sparkling. "If you'll follow me, ladies, our pickup will be merely a moment." We obediently hurry after him, my brain frantically trying to figure out what we're doing that gave us away.

He moves fast, and we have to almost trot to keep up. Surely we're gonna attract attention? When he turns the corner and we're out of sight of the soldiers, though, he spins on his heel and grins at us. "Wotcha, girls. I'm Leaf." The educated tones are totally gone, street cant thickening his voice and making him sound older, if a lot poorer. I open my mouth to speak, but he holds a finger up, waggling it. "No time for that. Sol-patrol's comin' around in five, had to bust ya outta there before they come through. We gotta bit of a walk in front of us. Hope you're in good shape!" He clips off the earpiece—an elaborate fake, I now see. So, no ride. I hesitate, thinking. Sol-patrol...Soldier patrol? We're already running? Rolling my eyes at Abial, I open my mouth to ask for a sit rep, but the boy is already retreating down the road, and the dull thud of military boots stepping in time becomes audible around the corner. I shut my mouth with a snap and bolt after the weird kid, wishing I'd been allowed to wear boots instead of flimsy, impractical shoes. I feel every irregularity in the street surface, and the warning burn of future blisters is already bothering me.

We travel rapidly, and every time he can't avoid a soldier group, Leaf takes on his "gentleman" air again, so rapidly it's hard to follow. He's a chameleon, switching from one personality to another without a pause, altering everything about the way he carries himself—even his facial expressions. It's a dislocating sensation to watch it happen, let alone try to keep up with.

We're running, and then suddenly walking at a gentle pace, admiring the scenery and being regaled with the backstory of particular buildings, and then abruptly running again. The impromptu tour is actually quite interesting. I've only been into Fourth City twice now, as it's dangerous for untrained Psionics to leave the slums, and learning about Second City is almost as good. Apart from a slightly different layout, it's difficult to tell them apart. And, under the guise Leaf has chosen for us as tourists, I gape up at the towering buildings to my heart's content. It does go on for longer than I'd want, though. It's getting dark, and I'm extremely hungry by the time he stops.

He glances back and forth, then leans casually on the wall, evidently waiting for a gap in pedestrians. Wondering where we are, I look around and see we're in a narrow street bracketed by closed shops. The stores around us are only two stories tall, unlike most of the City. I see a cam on the building opposite, although we're positioned right outside of its line of sight. It'll be impossible to avoid all the security cameras, but I appreciate the idea of keeping my face off as many as possible, especially if we're about to do something like...oh, break into a building. I duck a bit farther back into the shadows, then turn to see Leaf squatting in front of a door. He rustles for a few minutes, setting my teeth on edge, although Abial looks perfectly relaxed, as if she knows exactly what's going on.

It's annoying, and I'm about to ask what's taking so long, when I hear the familiar sound of an electric lock disengaging, and Leaf opens the front door of what looks like a store that's gone out of business. Thick metal shutters guard the large window facing the street, and the door appears sturdy, I note approvingly. It should do for a place to hide while we try to find out what's going on. Now we're in the City, I hope we can access news feeds holding information—at least what the public's been told. Leaf might know something useful, as well. We need any kind of insight at this point. It's hard to make a plan without intel.

Night has crept up on us, and the sky is almost totally dark. I glance down the road one more time, then follow Abial and Leaf into the building, eager to get off the streets and to work. Shutting the door behind me, I turn to check out the place.

Leaf waves a hand dramatically. "Here we go, folks. The owner got arrested two weeks ago, but they ain't showed anyone new around yet, so I took a look-see, and I reckon it'll be a suitable base for ya." There's a note of pride in his voice, and suddenly he appears older again, holding his body differently and looking even less the young gentleman, more a ruffian in his late teens. He runs his fingers through his hair, disrupting the harsh style it was combed into, and grins broadly at us, looking rather devilish with the sharp shadows on his angular face. "Yeah, looks good."

I stop looking around the shadowy room and grin back at him. "Smart move, thanks. We thought we'd have to base in the townships, but this'll work much better, long's no one comes looking to move in." I absently run my fingers over the frame on a dark workstation.

The room is large and narrow, with workstations on both sides, and full of large shelves running the length of the place. Good for hiding behind if anyone comes poking around. Maybe this used to be a gamer cafe, or similar. There's a door leading to another dark room, and stairs disappearing through a cutout in the low ceiling. More hiding spots. I nod at Leaf, appreciative he's found a spot we can use.

He nods back at me, as if he's agreeing he's done a good job. "Nah, love. They have to list it on the street census if there's to be a new business, or what have ya. Don't turn lights on at night or nothin' stupid, though." I shoot him a withering look he merely grins cheekily in response to, and then I realize Abial's already setting up the datapad for long comms, checking in with the base. Leaving her to it, I have a little poke around, discovering the door leads to a small kitchen with its own exit—great if we have to leave in a hurry. Loping up the stairs, I discover a good-sized attic still packed with boxes. It has windows at both ends which could also be used as emergency exits if necessary.

Padding back down, I undo the tight City hairstyle, which is starting to itch behind my ears. "This is great, Leaf. Thanks. So, what do you know about all the new soldiers coming off the tube? Are they coming from other Cities as well? Where're they heading?" I want to ask who he is, how he knows Kion, and what he's planning on helping us with, but there are more pressing issues at hand. If someone's on the run right now, we don't have a lot of time for chatting. It's enough that he's here; I quash my curiosity for now.

"My baby bro's been stalking their captain for me. They've been jumpin' all over, settin' up raids, flattenin' anyone who gets in the way. But they ain't found whatever they're lookin' for yet. I tell ya, I ain't never seen a hive so worked up. And I nick stuff from them all the time, so I should know!"

He nicks stuff from them? How does he get away with it? I tilt my head, and for the first time since leaving the safety of the ARC base, I spread my Talent out a little, looking for his mind. He grins wolfishly at me, appearing to know what I'm doing, and I sigh. "Total Blank, eh?" That explains it. I can't sense his thoughts even a little; he's impenetrable, invisible to mental probes. If he weren't Talented, I'd be able to read every last part of his current thoughts and feelings. If he were deliberately shielding, I might only get a fleeting impression, but I'd be able to sense at least an awareness of his presence. But Leaf may as well not be standing in front of me at all. To my power, he doesn't exist. A gap where there should be a person. Unreadable, unknowable.

He smirks, eyes crinkling up behind his now-disheveled fringe. "That's why I'm useful!" He's right; Blanks, those immune to psionic interference, make great spies. Without physically seeing them, there's no way of knowing where they are or where they've been. I'd wager they're immune to mind wipes as well, but I have no idea if I'm right. Leaf must be pretty damn good if he can steal things from right under the Institute's nose, as a Blank. But didn't I just see him take on two totally different personas so well I couldn't even pinpoint all the things he changed? Body posture, facial tension, expressions, even the way he looks around now is edgier, less refined. No wonder he's a talented thief. A Blank with great acting skills is pretty much perfect for a criminal career. I blow air out through my nose, impressed despite myself, and lean against a convenient table. I hope he's willing to put those skills to use for us. We'd stand a better chance with anyone who knows the area, so someone with his talents would be a gift from Google.

"So, are you just setting us up with our digs, or are you sticking around to help us out?" The question isn't a challenge. The mission brief we received merely said one of Kion's contacts would pick us up and help us find our feet. I fully expect Leaf will leave us to it, sooner or later, but he doesn't seem to be in a hurry. At the workstation, Abial is typing away rapidly, chatting to base, no doubt. I continue to ignore her, more concerned with Leaf, for the moment, than what base has to say. After all, for all intents and purposes, we're on our own. Base can't help us anymore. Leaf might be able to, though. And I'll take what I can get.

"Well, I'll stick aroun', show ya where the boys've been, pick up stuff if ya need it. But I'm not lookin' to get in no fights. This body were made for lovin', not wrestlin'." He unfurls a slow smile at me and lifts his eyebrows suggestively. I shoot him a long, cold stare until he deflates. Seriously, kid? He has a lot to learn if he thinks a smile's gonna get him in my shock suit. Besides, I bet he'd wet himself if I offered to take him up on his offer, not that I would. Boys. Not my thing. Despite myself, I glance at Abial again before replying.

"We're here on business. We'll take whatever you have to offer, but keep your eyebrows and everything else to yourself. Deal?" He snorts a laugh and hops up on a table, propping his elbows on his knees and tugging his earlobe absentmindedly.

"Alright, Tiger. Sheathe them claws. I ain't a twist. Whaddya need?"

Abial looks up from the datapad and brushes her hair out of her eyes, the darkened room partially obscuring the details of her features. For a minute, she's a stranger rather than one of the most familiar faces in my life. It's as though Abial has changed on the inside—hardened, perhaps—and the shadows are highlighting the difference.

But the moment breaks when she speaks. "We need food and water, for sure. Weapons if you can get 'em. It'd be good to get different clothes. We might need disguises, but that depends on what kind of plan we come up with. Come and look at this map and show us what's been going on." Her tone brooks no argument, and Leaf slides off the table gracefully. He might not be a fighter, but he's got the body and poise of a dancer, with lean muscles visible under his well-cut suit, and surprisingly solid pectorals for his slender frame. I shift position so I can see better too.

Abial clicks the projector on, and with a few gestures, has a holographic bird's-eye view of the city floating in the air. Around Leaf's waist. He smirks and moves a little, then points to a spot directly in front of his hips. "Tallest buildin' in the city." He snickers, but Abial clears her throat, obviously not amused, and he backs up until he's no longer surrounded by the hologram. I stifle a grin, more entertained by the flirty banter when it's not directed at me.

"Right, well. Can I mark this? Might be easier." Abial offers him a flat rectangular box, and he dips his index finger into it, pressing the pad firmly against the small, clear disc sparkling there. Now, when he gestures over the map, a line will follow in the wake of his finger. He taps his finger and thumb together, obviously familiar with the device, then starts drawing yellow Xs on the map. I shuffle closer and look on with interest, feeling my features settling into a focused expression, teeth worrying at my bottom lip as I concentrate. We're in a difficult situation, any intel we gather now might be the difference between life and death. We need to know where they've been, for how long, and where they're headed. We can't just stumble around in the dark hoping to happen upon whatever they're looking for. We've gotta figure out what they're doing.

By the time I'm ready to pay attention, Leaf's marked crosses and an erratic red line across the map. "Okay, so the soldiers've all been movin' down this line, with for-sure incidents where I done the crosses." I struggle to make sense of his slang and then laugh to myself. Why does he use a ridiculous accent when he's clearly capable of speaking properly? The points he's marked on the maps are probably what he mentioned earlier—the raids.

"Oh yeah, where you done them. I see," I tease him, smiling when he shoots an unheated glare at me. He grins back wickedly, then shrugs a shoulder in an eloquent lack of explanation and turns back to the map. There are now four yellow crosses on the holograph, while the red line trails from the Wall and meanders randomly—as far as I can tell— across the City. If that's where the soldiers are focused, it seems probable they're following someone who knows the City fairly well—someone who's moving on a strange route to avoid the solar panels streets, by the looks of things.

Leaf flicks the drawing disc back to Abial, who catches it with telekinesis and pops it back into the case it came from while I draw my own conclusions. The soldiers are scrambling, reacting. Good for us, I guess. Although it might make them difficult to avoid. "Have you seen or heard anything about what they're after, what this is all for?" I peer over the map, flicking it with my finger so it spins in the air, then pinching so it zooms in on the first yellow cross. "What happened here?" I'm starting to get a headache and scrunch my forehead in the hopes of warding it off.

"Power out, which hardly ever happens in the City, as I bet ya know. Cut for six blocks, then another section went dark a few minutes later. Soldiers pitched up pretty fast. I followed them 'cuz they rumbled right pas' where I was doin' a job. I was sneakerin' like, not that they woulda noticed if I'd joined in and started marchin' right along with them. They're all too busy checkin' their 'quip and chattin' back ta base about a breach. They were panickin'. Whatever they're after they want it pretty bad. Get?"

I shuffle smoothly onto a handy desk and settle in, gesturing for him to continue. I do indeed "get." There's a big palaver over Google knows what, and something that's caused a huge power cut, which is totally weird. Plus, soldiers heading around the city like ants from a damaged hive. I sigh, pinching the bridge of my nose. Okay, we can do this. We've gotta figure out where the soldiers are, not go there, and somehow get ahead of them to find the target. Easy. Internal sarcasm aside, this is obviously not gonna be a cut-and-dried mission. I wish someone else was with us, someone else to spitball ideas with. Having Leaf around is relieving a bit of the tension between Abial and me, but it would be a huge load off to have Kion, or anyone, really, to brainstorm with.

Meanwhile, Abial continues to make notes as Leaf spins the map so he can point out a building at the first yellow cross. "I chatted brief with the body who owns this apartuh." His pronunciation of "apartment" is weird enough to make Abial snort a little huff of air out of her wide nose, but he pays no attention to her and continues with his story, clearly completely comfortable with his bizarre way of speaking. I like him, I decide. He's a silly little toe rag, though. He's also taking entirely too long to tell us what we need to know.

"All right, can we get to the point? Clock's ticking..." Leaf looks slightly hurt but continues at a faster pace.

"And he said before the place went dark, two soldiers had demanded he shut his buildin' down, hard. No one in or out. So they're after a body. Ain't been able to hear any description, or nothin' helpful, though. The soldiers were diggin' round in that buildin' for hours, but when they went, they only left a two-man guard. They booted back ta their base, clearly on a dead trail. Then I guess they got more orders, or a clue as ta what they were after, 'cuz they kicked off again and done more buildin's like the first. They're still guardin' the empty buildin's, but not heavy-like, and no one's been allowed back in. I could get ya in if ya want a look-see yerselves?"

"Huh. But they're just hopping from building to building, shutting stuff down and not caring that the Citizens are getting creeped out? Weird. Is there an official story?" I ask, steepling my small hands in front of my face, elbows resting on knees. I'm confused and a little out of my depth, but I'm determined not to show it.

"Stuff on the wire is all 'terrorist this, terrorist that.' They never come up with anything new, do they?" Abial replies, clicking her fingers together furiously, text streaming over the top of the holograph. "According to this news site, there's a dangerous terrorist on the loose who's stolen something important from the governor. No information about what it could be—not that I'd believe it anyway—but there's a reward offered for any information." Her voice is terse and professional, and I breathe out slowly, thinking.

"Well they've obviously lost something. And whatever it is that's gone, and whoever it is that stole it, we want them. Obviously. Is there any pattern to the buildings the soldiers have been attacking? Anything we can use to predict where this mystery character might go next?" I run my fingers through my hair, getting caught up in the problem, and zoom in and out on the map to check for information about the locations. Apart from the fact that they're in a sort of line, jagged though it is, I can't work out why they've been chosen. They look totally random—starting with a storage facility, then an apartment, then a factory. None of them are owned by the same people, according to the info Abial is pulling up and flicking onto the holo for us to read. I rack my brain for reasons I would choose a place if I was on the run and frown.

There's not enough information. "Leaf, can you find out if anything else happened while you've been with us?" Only a few hours, but maybe an update will make it clearer.

Leaf fires off a message on his comm and we wait.

# Part Five

# Sam

I HOLE UP in the loading dock of a food warehouse—one of those that distributes foodpacks to the local businesses and schools. There are people around, but I manage to slip past a truck and worm my way into a huge pile of storage pallets, trying not to touch anything with my bare skin. I'm buzzing with a powerful elation at having managed to pull off a move I've only seen in the movies.

My shoulder is killing me, but I'm so excited to see what I've managed to steal in the bag I barely notice it, my blood singing and hot in my veins. I hope whatever I've got is going to help me. Feeling as if I'm on overload, I force myself into a small space and unzip the bag, squinting to make out what's inside in the darkness. I grope through, finding dozens of palm-sized pieces of squashy plastic secured in a rack and currently inert, with no electronics or machinery of any kind embedded in them.

I can't figure out what the squashy plastic pieces are, so I move them to one side and grab the next item. As soon as my fingers close on it my stomach unknots. A datapad. Finally. An interface I can use to find out what the Institute knows so I can start to plan with real information, instead of relying on what's flying around me in the air at any given time. I clutch it to my chest and realize I'm crying when a drop of water hits the back of my hand. Embarrassed, I sniff and wipe my face, looking around like there's anyone in this tiny space to laugh at me.

The bag doesn't yield any food or drink, sadly, but it does give me a padded box of what might be fuses with a pinlight on the top, a couple of power packs for a Zap gun—useless to me—and finally a spare T-shirt. I wish for a pair of pants, since I'm running around wearing what basically amounts to a paper skirt on my bottom half, but I'm out of luck there.

The datapad, however, could be the difference between life and death. But first things first. I have to find out where they're holding my mother. I have to get her out. It's laughable, acting as if I'm a one-man army, like I can walk in there, guns blazing, and rescue her. But I don't know what else to do, and getting information is as good a place as any to start.

The datapad whirs to life with a sound like breathing, like a heartbeat. Like love. I've never been so disconnected for so long, and my skinny fingers cradle the precious machine as the screen flickers on. I disable the location lock with half a thoughtform, telling it to send out its last location on the opposite side of the City and then stop reporting. The screen is Institute issue, and all the apps appear to be fairly standard: G-maps, internet, protocol, paperwork submission, handbook, messaging, images, calendar, settings, a calculator, and nothing else.

Makes no difference to me. I eagerly dive into the internet and navigate to the "place" where I store all my stuff. It takes seconds to pull an image of my powerful software—the one I've spent years designing in every spare moment—onto the datapad, which darkens for a moment as new programming wipes out the old.

Then I'm in my world. I have threads set up to every major organization I might ever want to look into, and yes, that means the Institute. I've never dared to venture far in before, in case they somehow traced me back, but I don't care anymore. I'll go in, and even if they notice, I can't be in more trouble than I am already. File options scroll up on screen, and I run search protocols for my name, my ID number, and my mom's.

The advanced software doesn't help the machine work any faster, as the hardware isn't made for this, and long moments spool out while I bite the skin on the edges of my fingernails into bloody tatters. To kill the time, I search a picture of the weird things I found in the bag with the datapad and discover that they're plastic explosives, fuses detached.

Eyes wide, I quickly read an idiot's guide to using them—I can't imagine wanting to, but if worse comes to worst, I guess I'd rather go boom than be taken in. A Zap would make it easier, but I don't have one. Once I'm sure I have the fairly simple instructions committed to memory, I have nothing to do again but wait.

Then the machine gives a soft *ping* and a folder pops up. Christina Dovzhenko, deceased. Sensation drains from my face, and I drop the datapad, my mouth falling open, nausea swamping me and sending my vision sparkling into spots. Distantly, I feel the sharp corners of plastic pressing into my back as I collapse. Christina Dovzhenko, deceased. Bile fills my mouth, sharp and bitter. I gag, cough it out. Christina Dovzhenko, deceased.

*No.*

My breath comes in heaving, painful little sips, not giving me enough oxygen. My head is too heavy, bobbing on my weak neck, and I clap my hand to my chest as shooting pain bursts through my sternum. I'm having a heart attack. I think it distractedly, not able to care intellectually, but my body feels as if it's seizing. My rib cage is too small, my stomach sloshing and burning, throat closed, and hot tears streaking over my face to fall unhindered.

The feelings come in waves I can't fight off. I'm helpless and fragile as my body shakes in rejection and distress, and I end up curled against the pallet, hugging my knees and crying in huge, wretched sobs.

I cry myself out, dehydration and shock warring to finally leave me empty and wrung out. My eyes are gritty and tender, my limbs shaking feverishly, and my skin too hot and tight for my body. Christina Dovzhenko, deceased. She's dead. How can she be dead? I should look in the file, but I'm afraid. Maybe if I don't see the evidence, then it won't be true—a horrible mistake has been made. They're trying to trick me so I'll cave in, give up.

I'm numb, hollow as if someone has reached inside me and scraped my organs from my shell. My mother. My only real family, my best friend and confidant. Memories wash over me, begging for my attention, threatening to unravel me again—but I shove them away, welcoming the numbness, the absence of feeling.

Robotically, I reach for the datapad. I'm going to ruin them. The thought uncurls in my stomach, a small burn of rage replacing the emptiness. Before, I only wanted to get away, to leave this place and start over. But now I know what they've done. They've killed my mother, and they have to pay. They have to suffer.

Without really thinking about it, I plug myself back into their systems, this time with a more specific purpose. It takes me some time to get through their outer layers of protection, and I hear engines warming up and trucks driving in and out of the warehouse I'm hidden in while I work. It's nothing but background noise. I ignore it and run through cyberspace, through the inner workings of the Institute, looking for evidence of their crimes. Slave files. Obituary reports. Films of interrogations. I'm going to take all their dirty laundry and unleash it on the world. I will tatter their security and expose them for what they truly are. Monsters in the guise of men.

Hours pass as I collate more and more data, more instances of terror and harm. I'm sick to my stomach with the indignities I'm exposed to. Children taken from hospitals at birth, swapped out for untalented babies. Memories absorbed and wiped clean until they're robot people blindly obeying an organization they have been programmed to love and respect. Deaths. Abductions. Abandonments. Abuse.

It blurs together into a never-ending waterfall of evil, spanning generations, weaving back through the history of our nation. There's no space inside me for the breadth of desecration I'm viewing. Power. It all comes back to power—holding on to it and pushing down those who are at the bottom in order to keep themselves on top.

The datapad eventually flickers and dies, battery utterly drained by my activities. It shakes me back to the real world. I'm cramped and starving, I realize. Empty of energy and hope. I shouldn't have stayed this long; if anyone has noticed my incursion into the secrets of the Institute, they might be able to backtrack to my location. I need to keep moving, but in my distress, I wasn't thinking clearly. Resolute, I stuff the datapad into the bag and get to my feet.

Well, I try. What actually happens is that my legs, totally asleep after hours squashed into an extremely uncomfortable position, politely refuse my suggestion that we get to our feet, and topple me sideways in a pile of pallets. The noise is deafening and my heart sticks in my throat, choking me as I angrily try to rub sensation back into my recalcitrant limbs. Pins and needles flare viciously in my calves and feet, and I bite my lip to keep from crying out as I pummel them. Come on, come on! I think, terrified.

Finally tottering upright and slinging the bag over my shoulder, I grab onto the edges of the pallets to help support me and squirm gracelessly through the precarious stacks. It's a good job I'm basically malnourished and short. An average-sized adult man would never be able to worm his way through here.

I snake myself around the piles, getting progressively more claustrophobic and eventually realizing I have no way of knowing if I'm even headed for open space. I could be about to trap myself against a wall. Cursing my lack of forethought, I keep going. It gradually gets lighter as I wriggle past bruising corners and scratching edges, and, on the theory that light is probably not coming from a warehouse wall, I try to work my way closer to the source of it.

To my relief, I find myself almost in a corner, but facing out onto the warehouse floor itself. I see maybe a dozen uniformed figures stacking, moving pallets on forklifts, and piling crates in the back of open vans. Thankfully, no one seems to have noticed my crash and bang back in the stacks, the hum of engines and clatter of huge boxes being moved presumably covering it up.

I hear a voice right next to me and I flinch backward in shock. Somehow I manage not to knock anything over in my surprise but freeze as the woman yells, "Gherk, bring the damn truck back. I ain't gonna lug these all the way over the floor."

Gherk, whoever he is, grunts an affirmative, and one of the vans starts reversing. The woman hauls open the doors, which are about six feet away from the stacks I stand in, and I blink. If I worm along a bit, I can make a run for it and get into the van. I'd be past the security here, and be moving all day, hopefully. With a bit of luck, I'll be able to stay ahead of the Institute. I mean, why would they look for me in a food delivery truck?

And I'm uncomfortable with the idea of staying here any longer. My innards are churning with misery, and I'm too foggy to figure out a better plan. At least if I'm in the van, I can hunker down and still be on the move. The woman is already loading pallets onto the moveable hydraulic shelf at the back of the vehicle, piling them up. If I'm going to go, it has to be now. I glance around, desperately hoping no one is looking in my direction.

They're not. I squirm sideways, until I'm almost directly behind the vehicle, and wait for my moment. The woman turns to answer a yell from the other side of the warehouse, peering around the side of the parked van, and I swallow my fear determinedly as I slip out into the open space. One stumble could ruin me. The workers would probably kick me out onto the streets at best, hold me for the Watch at worst.

I make it in five steps, my muscles trembling from too much sitting, followed by physical exertion. Then I bash my shin into the floor of the van as I scramble past the pallets and move to squat behind them, clammy and nauseous. Pressing myself against the metal sheet dividing the storage section from the cab, I tremble and wait for the shouts of discovery. But nothing comes. The rest of the area is filled, leaving me with barely enough room to breathe at the back of the unit, and then the engine rumbles to life. We're off.

If the Institute tracks me to the warehouse, they might figure out I got in a van, but they'd still have to check the dozens heading in and out of there. The spur-of-the-moment nature of my idea to get in helps, because I know for sure I didn't leave the thought embedded on a surface for them to pick up.

THE DAY PASSES in a haze of misery and exhaustion. I nod off without meaning to, jerking awake when the van bumps to a halt every now and again. Eventually, I wake and everything is quiet and still. The pallets are gone; the van is empty.

How did I escape discovery? Maybe no one looked in the van after the last sheet was out. Maybe I looked like a heap of crumpled clothes, or a dead body. Maybe they're calling the Watch right now. I slither across the hard metal paneling to the door and grab the handle, then take a deep breath. If they're waiting for me, there's nothing I can do. I could disable their Zaps, but is there even any point? Wouldn't it be better to die here rather than being taken to the Institute, to live an unlife, robbed of myself? I trickle my power out slowly and hunt for any sign of electronics, but all I can sense is electric lighting—off, a computer unit or two, and the wiring running through every wall.

But just because I can't sense a dozen weapons aimed at me doesn't mean the soldiers aren't there. Maybe they've finally caught on to my skillset. I'm geek boy, tech head, any one of the nicknames the kids at school use. They could have everyone on "dark protocol"—no electronics or technology, ready to hit me in the head with a baton.

My stomach knotting painfully, I wrap my long fingers around the plastic handle. The material digs into the tendons in my digits as I yank it open. It moves easily, the van's not a jail truck, after all, and I tumble out, ready to make a run for it, and actually sprint a few steps on unsteady legs before realizing I'm alone.

There's no one in the vast warehouse. Only me, surrounded by more food than I'd ever be able to eat, if only I could get to it without a crowbar.

Thrusting the thought away, I pad across the cold concrete to the control room, where I sense the computers, and try the door. It's locked, obviously; I didn't expect anything different. But there's a big viewing window so whoever's in there during the day can see out into the room. If I want to spend the night anywhere except this warehouse, I need to get in there. I'll never be able to bust out of the huge metal sliding doors guarding the loading bay, so it's the smaller room or nothing.

The transparent aluminum is cold as I press my cheek against it, peering inside and trying to make sense of the shapes in the darkness. The only light comes from the window I'm looking through and the cracks around the other door, which leads out of the room in the opposite direction.

My face squashed as close as possible, I look for a way in. I could try to get out of the warehouse, go around and try the other door, but... Then I see it. A black shape sticking out of the door close to me, at key height. They've left the key in there! And thanks to far too many hours watching television, I know how to get the key to this side of the door if it's in the keyhole.

Excited, I spin around and dash across the room to look for the things I'll need. Moments later, I'm back, armed with a piece of wire I found discarded on the floor and a sheet of fiberpaper containing today's, or maybe yesterday's, news. I shove the paper under the door, using the gap where it doesn't quite sit flush with the ground, and then carefully push the wire into the keyhole. I wiggle it around for a few moments, and then it gives, and there's a clanking sound on the other side of the door.

I scramble to my feet and press myself against the window again, crossing my fingers. The key has landed half on, and half off, the paper. Anger surges in me, but I squash it back down. Throwing myself to the ground, I hold my breath and delicately pull the paper back through, toward me. The key catches on the door, too wide for the gap, though, and I wiggle the paper sideways in hopes of finding a bigger space without losing the key entirely.

When the end of the metal object finally peeps out from under the metal door, I place my finger on the tiny sliver visible and slowly stroke it through, millimeter by millimeter, pulling the paper at the same time.

Once half the key is on my side, I pinch it between finger and thumb and tug it the rest of the way in a rush until it's clutched in my sweaty hand. Success! Buoyed by victory, I shove the key into the keyhole, twist it, and burst into the room. The computer here is big, powerful. It's connected to the main power lines for the City and will, at last, provide me with hardware matching my software capabilities. If I want to get the information I've found into the world, show everyone the depravities of the Institute, I need to steal it and upload it. It would take time and more processing power than a small unit can muster. The kind of power you find in a factory control system!

I swiftly link the datapad I've been using to the big desktop and use them in tandem. Retracing my steps from earlier, finding the videos, the files, I download them as I go and then hide the information in my secret corner of the nets, the datapad charging up as I trawl through cyberspace. Using this beast of a desktop is so much easier, so much faster. While the data I've stolen uploads, I quickly download a map of the City's original power lines, looking for buildings I can use in this same way. Steal their info, hide it, and then...the coup de grâce. Hack the City and replace the propaganda, the advertisements, and the newsfeeds with a self-edited film, show everyone what's really happening in the City.

I cross-reference my list of buildings with hours of operation for the businesses which work out of them, and then with security blueprints and passcodes. After an hour, I think I'm sufficiently prepared.

I leave the warehouse via the main exit, courtesy of a handful of keys from the office. I'd feel almost jaunty, now I have a plan and a purpose—but my mother is dead, and I have the most terrifying branch of the government breathing down my neck. I find a change of clothes on a washing line, yank a pair of pants on without even taking my shoes off, then stuff my hands in the pockets, trying to look busy as I head for my next target. Stay ahead of them. No more than one hour in each location. They don't know what I'm wearing, or what I'm doing.

I can do this.

# Serena

WE WAIT, AND when Leaf's comm beeps, he gestures for the drawing chip again and adds a few more crosses placed farther and farther away from the original incident. He wriggles his nose from side to side, swooping eyebrows narrowed in concentration. Then he brightens suddenly, straightening up and waving a hand in the air to get our attention. "They're all wired!" he exclaims, excitement filling his hushed voice. "All the new buildings're on the original wire trunk, holdin' massive servers. Maybe the terrorist chap needs a pluggable connex for somethin', not just wireless. Look!" He takes the datapad right out of Abial's hands so quickly she's still blinking at the empty space where it was, when he starts typing away on the touchscreen, pulling up and discarding things so rapidly I can't even make out what they are. Pickpocket. I'd bet on it.

I smirk at Abial's shocked expression. Usually she's the fastest at everything and clearly Leaf's speed has thrown her off. My attention is pulled back by Leaf's voice and I look back at him. "Aha!" He taps again, and the city map is overlaid with a blueprint showing massive swathes of wiring under the city. The original underground power lines for the entire City's grid.

My eyes scan the map, and then the blueprint over it, heart racing. Leaf is right—every building hit is at a terminal point on the wires, meaning direct access to the City's power if you manually spliced in. Whoever we're chasing needs power, lots of it, for whatever they're doing. Leaf pauses, his face suddenly growing serious, concern painting his features. "Nuke! If I figured it out this fast, either the soldiers are thicker'n rocks, or they know too."

"And they're almost certainly already on their way to the next stop." I finish his thought for him, mind flashing through the possibilities. Whoever this person is, they're taking a traceable route. The soldiers have to be on to it, which means they're probably heading toward the next building. If we're gonna get there first, we don't have much time. I nod, pursing my lips. "You're right. There's no way they missed this. Not with the sort of tech they're running. Look, there's three buildings that make sense as a next stop, and four more a little farther out if this person is willing to move an extra klick. So she could be hiding in any one of these seven locations!"

"She?" Leaf raises a sharp eyebrow, eyes glittering like oil. "Why she?"

I smirk, raising an eyebrow back at him. "Why not? Anyway, if they're sending the Institute scrabbling, it doesn't matter who they are. Just that we get to them first. They've got to be important, and that means we need them."

Abial scrapes her hair off her face, pulling it into a firm horsetail. "Right, we're gonna need an evac plan, and a safe house other than this one. Can't risk coming back to the same place. I vote we get some food, put a plan together, and bounce ASAP. If you guys are right, we don't have much time." She slaps her hand on her hip to check her Zap, then realizes she isn't wearing it, and sighs. "Weapons would be nice too. Leaf, could ya try to pull something together for us?"

But he's already sliding toward the door, moving like silk. He pats his hair back into place, and suddenly the guttersnipe is gone, replaced by a self-confident, affected young gentleman. The chameleon effect is impressive; I'd never guess he was the same pickpocket who's been entertaining us for the past ten minutes. He grins, and the mask disappears for a second. Then he listens at the door, waits a few beats, and slips out without a sound.

There's a moment of silence, and then Abial breaks it. "He's kinda creepy." I blurt a laugh at the idea of Abial being creeped out by our new friend. She's usually so unflustered, taking everything in her stride—something I've always been envious of.

"Eh, pretty neat trick, changing it up like that. I wonder if he can do any other characters. Maybe he can give us some pointers." Then I jerk my head at the map. "We'd better get to it. Like you said, we don't have much time." We settle in at the workstation, anchoring the holo map to the wall so we can refer to it as we start pulling information from the city archives and nets, working together to formulate a plan that will get us to the right place and then out of the City. Preferably with our lives intact.

WHEN LEAF COMES back, he slips down the stairs at the side of the room without making any sound whatsoever, scaring the nuke out of me. A slight change in the room alerts us, and we whirl simultaneously, thrusting power at him. I intended to slam the intruder into the wall, but he merely slides sideways, untouched, and snickers, raking his now-messy hair off his forehead again.

My heart is in my throat, hands outstretched from the failed attack. Blanks are notoriously difficult to affect with telekinesis. Without the implicit understanding of their body position that comes with the reading of minds, it's almost impossible to wrap mental "muscles" around them. Which means half of my martial training is useless against him. That pisses me off, as well as the fact he caught us by surprise when we're supposed to be on high alert. "Blank or no, you'd be a splat on the wall if we had Zaps, idiot," I snarl at him, dropping my hands and turning back to the datapad I've been using to familiarize myself with all possible routes to the sites we've designated as likely targets. He doesn't wilt under the hard stare he's receiving from Abial, I note, watching from the corner of my eye as I pretend my muscles aren't juddering from the rush of adrenaline.

Instead, he just chuckles again. "Nah if ya had Zaps, I'd have taken the back door and disarmed ya before ya got a shot off at me."

"Or you could have knocked like a normal human being." Abial's tone is scathing, but a smile lurks around the corners of her mouth. I scowl at her; my own hackles are still up, I'm totally on edge, but Abial appears to be over it already, only serving to irritate me more. Doesn't she think we should be taking this a little more seriously?

Leaf hops up onto a handy set of plastic crates and grins broadly at us both, clearly pleased by our reactions. "Well, that'd only work if we had a secret knock, wouldn't it? Else ya'd never have answered. 'Cuz yer not supposed to be 'ere."

His matter-of-fact ridiculousness breaks through my frustration, and I sigh, throwing my hands up in defeat in the face of his unshakable smugness. "Fine, sneak in, make us *trained soldiers* jump, but don't come complaining if we accidentally hurt you. Deal?" I stare him down, deadly serious. It won't do any good if we accidentally crippled or killed our only ally in this City, but we'll need at least some cooperation from him to keep from doing that.

"If ya got extremely lucky!" He looks so unbearably cocky that I clench my fist and use my powers to yank the crate he's sitting on forward. He lurches, teetering dangerously before regaining his balance, and purses his mouth in wry acknowledgement. Point made, I shove the crate back into its place telekinetically and raise an eyebrow at him in challenge.

"Yeah, alright. I'll knock. Don't want ya throwin' a table at me, pretty face! What's the plan?" Satisfied he understands we're not here for fun and games, I lean on a table, waving my hand at Abial, who spins in her seat and gestures, bringing the map around so it's in front of her where Leaf can see it better. It's still vertical, though, and his face is lit up with an eerie blue as he leans in, emphasizing his rather feminine jawline and casting ghostly shadows that hide his eyes.

"As far as we can figure it, our best shot is to wait, find out where the soldiers are heading next, and then get there first. Knowing where they might be heading is all well and good, and if we had a whole crew we could hit up each joint at the same time, but we don't. So we have to beat the bad guys to wherever they're going. And then we should be golden. We're working on the assumption that someone has stolen something, and the Institute wants it back pretty badly, which means it could be able to damage them. It could be equipment, but it could also be intelligence. Anyway, the plan is to lend whoever they're chasing a hand, if we can and should, and then get them out of the City. Quick as we can. Without getting killed. Of course, if they don't want to cooperate, we might have to rethink our aims." Abial's face is hard in the cold lighting, and I twist my mouth unhappily.

We don't have a lot of good options, but kidnapping sounds a little too much like the methods the Institute uses. Whoever we're after might not welcome our help, and it's all too possible they won't want to go back to ARC at all. In which case, we'll have to relieve them of information and possible items. And I'm not exactly comfortable with the idea. But it would be irresponsible to leave a weapon able to help ARC behind, no matter the cost.

War brings impossible circumstances with it, and sometimes all the choices are bad, but I truly hope it doesn't come to hurting someone we could, instead, form an alliance with.

Whatever happens, I'll have to deal with it. This is the hand we've been dealt, and combat training has prepared us for high-risk situations. If we leave the person behind to be captured, it could compromise our chances of getting out of the City safely. And if either of us gets caught because the person we're chasing refuses to come with us, and knows too much—our minds will be plundered. That's why "Ways to Commit Suicide" is a class I've been taking since I was fourteen.

If we're out of touch for more than a day, the rotating entrances to the ARC headquarters will be destroyed, presumed compromised by our capture. Of course, we're not privy to much; ARC, by necessity, keeps information as compartmentalized as possible. In the hands of a skilled Reader, a captured operative might spell the end of the entire resistance. Taking my own life, if it comes to it, is something I think I've accepted. But murder? I push away the unwelcome thought that we may have to kill someone who could be an ally. There's no point in worrying before we even manage to catch up. Besides, I can't imagine being alone and hounded by the Watch and Institute alike and not wanting help. Everything will be fine. That's the idea for right now, and I'm sticking to it.

I clear my throat, wanting to pull Abial's thoughts away from killing. "They'll probably be happy to cooperate with anyone who can keep them alive. By the looks of the track so far, they're only one step ahead of the soldiers, meaning they're either hacking comms or the cameras to see where the bad guys are headed. If the Institute goes dark and turns off the city cams, whoever it is will be flying blind. They might end up surrounded without even realizing it. So we don't have much time. If I were in charge, it would already be a dark op, because it's so obvious the body they're after is tuned in to their approach."

A strange rumbling noise abruptly fills the room, interrupting me, and Abial and I react as the soldiers we are, immediately ducking and covering, hands up and looking for the source. Leaf balances, crouched on the crates, and when the sound comes again, louder this time, he leaps, catlike, to a less exposed position. I flick a thoughtform to Abial, adrenaline pumping through my veins, calling me to combat. *Explosions? Close! We need to get eyes on. Can you check the camera streams?*

*On it*, Abial responds tersely, tapping her fingers together without looking at her datapad, still scanning the room. All is quiet now, and Leaf slinks along the wall, pressing his eye to a crack in the metal-shuttered window. A strange pattering sound permeates the heavy silence, gradually getting louder, and then Leaf laughs, his whole body visibly relaxing. "It's a storm!" he crows over the noise, voice pitched perfectly to carry to us. I blink stupidly for a moment, and then my mouth drops open in surprise.

What? A storm? There hasn't been a rainstorm in over a decade! "No way!" I race over to Leaf, almost shoving him out the way so I can plaster my own eye to the crack. An actual storm! Nuke us all now? That's either the world's best or worst timing. It's gotta make it harder for cameras to pick anything out, and help to erase our trails... But it's also gonna make the trip a lot more unpleasant. "Oh, Google! This is incredible!" I hear the awe in my voice and feel the huge grin on my face. For a moment, I forget about the mission as I gaze into the streaming rain.

Outside, the City is suddenly bustling. The sunshields over the road are retracting automatically, sheets sliding over each other and sinking into waiting pods on the sidewalk. People are hauling covers from long-unused reservoirs on their roofs, and kids are already splashing in the rapidly forming puddles. The rain is heavy, and the roads start to flood, shining silver water slicking the solar panels. Abial pads over. "For real, a waterstorm?" She sounds equally excited, and I reluctantly move to let her take a look.

We stand for a few minutes, trading places to look through the gap in the shutters, and then Leaf clears his throat. "Should we, ya know, take advantage of the storm and get ta rescuin' yer damsel in distress? Might not have rained in eleven years, but I'm sure the bad guys ain't gonna stop blowin' stuff up so as they can splash in the puddles...." I sigh and nod, tucking my unruly hair behind my ear and already regretting my slip into childish excitement. I'm on a mission here, and if I mess it up, I could die. Along with the rest of the team, and possibly everyone back at home, if we really nuke it up.

Finally, satisfied I have my professional face back on, I clear my throat. "Yeah, you're right. So what did you score for us?" He slopes across the room and hauls a large duffel bag out from behind the stair railing; I assume he managed to put it down before we even heard him enter the room and puff air from my nose in unspoken admiration. Man, he's a ghost. Now in possession of the bag, he sits on the bottom stair with it between his legs and delves into it haphazardly. Abial catches my eye for a moment and we share a professional smile, but then Abial clearly remembers whatever has her so angry and looks away, slanting her gaze toward the ground.

I clench my jaw and squash the urge to physically shake the other girl until she gives up and tells me what the nuke is going on. Instead, I throw a thought at the sullen girl: *You need to get over it. We don't have time to hash it out, but we will... After this mission. I'm still the same person.* I keep my feelings locked down tight except for frustration.

Abial keeps her face studiously blank, ignoring the message. Leaf, oblivious to the interplay, is still rummaging. "'Nuff food for two days, 'nuff water for one, but we'll get ya set up somewhere ya can find fluid, 's too heavy ta carry any more. Ya can always drink the rain, anyhow." There's a laugh in his voice as he finishes and sets a few packages on the floor.

He tosses the next item out of the bag at me, quickly followed by one to Abial. We both field them easily, reflexes honed by hours of training, and I look. Zaps! Nice. "Pinched those from a Watch patrol 'cross town. They're registered, so ya'll have ta tinker with 'em, but I figured ya knew the rules when ya asked for 'em."

I grin in appreciation, holding the Zap up to get a good look at it. The handgrip is molded black plastic lined with strips of metal, gleaming dully in the gloom. On the side, a fingerprint reader is clearly visible in the depressions where a hand would curl around it. Abial beckons for me to pass mine over, and then sets them both on the table. She starts fiddling with them, attaching wires to the sensors, clearly not paying any more attention to Leaf and me as she works. I'm happy to leave her to it since I never excelled in the tech classes. Abial used to be a solar monkey, wriggling through the narrow passages under the roads to replace broken wires. She grew up with technology, and I know she can take care of it. Meanwhile, Leaf continues going through the bag, and I pad over so we can talk without disturbing Abial as she concentrates. I turn my attention to the ever-growing pile at Leaf's feet, hoping to see weapons and armor, in that order. We'll need them if we're gonna succeed on this mission.

Ten minutes later, I'm encased in the high-quality shock-pad armor he's brought. It's heavy and gelatinous, sculpted to my body shape and attached with a thin adhesive that disintegrates under UV. I've heard of it, but it's unfamiliar, enough that I need his help attaching the back piece and trimming the overly large edges.

When he's done, my whole torso is coated in a faintly gleaming, ominous-looking substance blending with the shadows behind me. I look at myself, twisting to and fro to check my flexibility. I'm practically invisible. I look amazing…er…professional. I clear my throat, wiping the happiness from my expression. "Pretty good. This is a quarter inch, right? Which means it'll stop penetration from anything more than forty-eight inches away, and decrease impact forces by five percent for each meter traveled prior to contact. Should be able to shrug off anything more than ten, fifteen meters!" I'm basically muttering to myself as I walk my fingers over the coating, but Leaf cocks his eyebrow at me anyway.

"I'd have just said 'This'll stop my insides from becomin' my outsides!' But I'm sure what ya said makes sense too."

I shrug at him, refusing to be embarrassed, and then pull my civilian long-sleeved brown shirt over the top. This time, I do the clips up all the way to my neck to hide the awesome black body armor underneath, then sigh, looking down at myself. "Well, I look like a lumpy prude, which I suppose is as good a disguise as any." I can't believe how thin the armor is—thinner than anything I've ever worn—and I press my hands against my belly, playing with the weird give of the flexible armor. It will harden instantly with impact, dispersing force across my torso instead of localizing the hit. It's pretty brilliant.

Abial chooses this moment to snap the power cell back into the Zap and flick it on, grabbing my attention. I literally feel my eyes widen as the grip turns red—usually a precursor to a localized explosion, which would render anyone stupid enough to try to use a registered Zap handless. I relax a second later, though, as no explosion follows, and the grip turns green. Abial flips it in the air and catches it with a solid thunk, grinning happily. My relief translates into a bit of silliness; for a moment I genuinely thought Abial was about to lose a hand. I jerk a thumb at her and smirk at Leaf. "She's the tech guy. I'm tactics."

He grins in response. "And I'm the tour guide. I get it. So, Tactics, what's the genius plan once ya find the feller in question?"

Genius plan...not much of one. But it's the best we can do. I finger comb my hair back and straighten my clothing over the armor, making sure it's unobtrusive. I start to put the gear Leaf brought into the small satchel that had held my "citizen" gear, which sits, abandoned, on the table. "We go and fetch, then we get out of the City. We're too easy to find here. If you can find us a place to go in the outer slums, we'll go there after we pick up the runner." I hope. "We've gotta be out of the City before dawn."

He furrows his brow at me. "Yeah, I got a place. You'll need coordinates and a knock rhythm. Here." He knocks out a pattern on the table, and I obediently copy him. I get it right the first time, and he gestures for me to repeat it. Smirking a little, I do so, getting it exactly right. Then he rattles off a list of numbers, which we both repeat back. The coordinates.

He snorts. "Very impressive. Shock me again, tell me how yer gonna get past the checkpoints on t' Wall." I grin slowly at him and jerk my hand at the altered Zap, which flies through the air and slaps into my waiting palm. A bit showy, sure, but I have the anticipation of a fight buzzing through me now, and my instincts are singing. I'm on edge, and it's making me act before I really think about it. Gotta stop that. Chill. At this rate, my power will be popping out of me.

Determined to get myself under control, I close my eyes for a second, then open them, refocused on our mission. I tuck the Zap into the back of my waistband and pull my civs over to cover it. "Ah, but we're not going through a check. We're going over it. And you'll be distracting the Institute while we do."

He blinks at me, lips parting in shock. "Over? Mercy, ya've gone plain cracked. How in the nuke're ya gonna get over?" Snickering, I fish the Watch communication unit he stole out of the pile and attach it to my wrist. I'm pleased with his reaction, enjoying unsettling him for some reason. Probably because he snuck in and made me jump, if I'm honest.

"Well, that's why I'm useful." I throw his earlier words back at him with a smug grin and fasten up the satchel. Over. We've never tried a telekinetic jump as high as this one will be, but with the two of us working together, I'm convinced we'll make it to the top of the forty-eight-meter Wall. We've practiced in the Arena, and all trainees learn how to propel yourself higher than should be possible, using your powers as a boost, shoving it out of the soles of your feet to launch you into the air. With the two of us combined, and the extent of Abial's power—and my own—we should be fine. Hopefully. Still, Leaf doesn't need to know the details. There's more than one way to extract information from someone, and just because he's a Blank doesn't mean he'd be able to stand up to torture. He's already got a lot of information about us, and the less he knows about our abilities, the better, all things considered.

Abial gets to her feet and cracks her neck from side to side, the sound sharp. Leaf winces and picks up the remaining shock pads. "Ya gonna put yer kit on, Lanky?" She shoots him a withering glance, then remarks casually to me, "How long do we have to put up with this warp?" But she grabs the pads from his outstretched hand. Excited to be getting underway, I laugh and wrangle the previously invisible straps out of the side of the flat satchel, then hoist it onto my back, where it lies neatly against my spine, out of the way and high enough it won't block my gun hand if I need to draw.

Then I pointedly glare at Leaf until he obediently spins on his heel, with a dramatic sigh, leaving me to help Abial put on the sticky-backed body armor. I'm about to unpeel the coating when I freeze, suddenly awkward. "Uh, do you want me to help?" What if she feels as though I'm taking advantage. Abial gives me an unreadable look and pulls her shirt off.

We've seen each other naked hundreds of times, but the huge scar covering Abial's right upper arm and shoulder in thick, raised whorls always chills me and makes me want to touch it in about equal amounts. She's tattooed over a lot of the damage—it's all black ink and pale scar and scraps of brown, healthy skin. The melted flesh is the result of a direct hit from a Zap during an Institute raid. The day Damon was taken. I thrust the memory away, concentrating only on the practicality of the matter at hand—applying the body armor inch by inch. My knuckle brushes her skin, and I flinch, then to break the awkwardness in the air, I reply to her question, even though several moments have passed. "Well, he's not coming with us for this bit, but I expect we'll keep in touch. Leaf, which part of the Wall is least heavily guarded?" The second pad, the front, is more difficult to apply, and I have to concentrate to get it to lie flat. Abial's tall enough, of course, that we won't have to cut it the way I did mine.

He scratches his jaw, leaning his other hand against the wall he's facing. "Uh, the East—not much town out there. S'desert almost immediately."

I squish together the edges of the body armor, where the pads meet on Abial's ribcage and flank. "Right, East's where we'll be exiting then. Which means we need a decent-sized explosion on the West, dig?" I pat Abial's shoulder to let her know she's done. Abial flexes and bends, then nods at me and starts getting her civilian kit back on.

"Yep, I gotcha. That means yer gonna have ta get across town from the northwest, where yer target's been dodgin'."

"I know. Leave it to us. You got a timepiece?" I bring up the clock on the new wrist unit and grimace; more time has passed than I thought, and we're gonna be cutting it close to get out of sight before we lose the cover of darkness.

"Call it an hour to get over there, maybe two to track the body down and get them out, another hour across town, and a half to be safe?" I don't pause long enough for anyone to give their opinion on my time estimates. "We'll be ready to go over at 00:30. If you pull off a big distraction at 00:15, it should give them enough time to call all the on-duty forces in..." I trail off, looking at his raised hand, and lift an eyebrow. "We're not in class. You don't have to put your hand up." Although I can't say I hate it.

He coughs, drops his hand a bit, and points to the comm he's wearing on his wrist. "This one's not just for show. Why don't ya comm me when yer ready ta rock? Wouldn't that be easier than all this 'set clocks ta synchronize at midnight when the crow flies east' stuff?"

Eech, he has a point. I blink and roll my eyes. "And if my comm breaks, or there's interference, or...all right, yeah. I'll comm you. But, if you haven't heard from me by midnight, blow something up anyway. Even if our mission breaks down, I like it when they have explosions to clear up. Gives them things to do. Hey, make sure it's civilian casualty-free though, aye?" If we die, at least Dad will see we didn't go quietly.

"Oh, don't worry, I'm gonna get my boys ta help me run game on City Hall. We'll take out a gatehouse or two; they'll think they're under full-on attack; we're shadows in the moonlight, an' all. Uncatchable mischief-makers. Ya'll get yer distraction. Ya got a map of the slums? I'll show ya where's best ta head. My da, Dent, and his mister'll put ya up 'til yer ready ta bust a move. And they're smugglers, so no probs hiding ya." Smugglers. Makes sense. Bet that's how he knows Kion, too. I know he's still in touch with the nomad tribes.

"Smugglers. Great. They'll probably make us lie under the floorboards and pretend we're sacks of grain," Abial mutters. "This all sounds like the best plan ever." Her sarcasm makes me frown. And how is attitude gonna help?

"We ready to bounce?" I inject false confidence into my question.

"Not yet. I gotta beep my boys." He starts tapping out a message at high speed, doing this—just like everything else—a little faster than looks normal. Then he taps his foot, pretending impatience as he waits for a reply, and grins when his comm lights up. "Nice. All ready? Reilly's on 'is way ta wipe the place down. He'll move the rest of this out for ya as well."

Right as he says it, his wrist unit flashes again, and he grins, pulling the door open a crack. A hasty exchange of muffled words is followed by a long-limbed blond man easing his way into the room. His clothes are a mottled gray-and-black streaky camo print, making him almost impossible to see, and he's dripping wet. I give him a quick once-over, noting his athletic build, raw-boned face, and deep-set brown eyes, darting around the room. He looks as though he's seen his fair share of fights, judging by the broken nose, but there's an intelligence in his features, I don't think this guy is only a thug.

He wrings his sleeves out briefly, the water pattering on the floor, and performs an elaborate bow. "Evening, ladies. I do 'ope this miscreant 'asn't tainted your visit to our fine city." He mournfully squeezes out his hair, and then sighs. "Lost cause. 'Ope you're prepared for a shower. S'unbelievable out there!"

I smirk and move toward the door, unable to keep the thrum of anticipation out of my voice. "Little water never hurt anyone. 'Sides, it'll help cover us. Dig your grays, by the way." I gotta get me some of those.

Water drips slowly off the end of his wide nose as he flashes a broad grin in reply. "Well, good luck in your endeavors. Don't worry about your prints. I'll scrub the place bare." He shrugs off a flat pack and unrolls it on the table, grabbing a small reader unit and clicking it on. The screen lights up and shows all the fingerprints and smears on the table in front of him. "And then I'll get some third-party contractors in to touch everything a bit. Nothing more suspicious than a well-cleaned joint. Freedom go with ya!" Satisfied he knows what he's doing, I watch interestedly as he sets to work, using a weird-looking cloth to clean the places we've touched. He whistles softly as he cleans, and Leaf claps him on the shoulder. "Later, Rei!" He sidles to the door, looks out, and grins at us. "Ready ta get wet?"

I nod eagerly, and we head into the maelstrom outside.

We're soaked immediately, and I'm grateful for the shock pads covering my torso, as they keep my chest and back dry. The rain isn't cold, but being drenched soon loses its novelty, and the visibility is terrible. Uneasy, I flick my gaze back and forth, tempted to use my power to read my surroundings. It's safer to keep it shut down, though, so I silently curse and resist.

We stay close together as we traipse through the already ankle-deep flooding. I miss my boots so much. Most of the civilians are inside by now, having opened their reservoirs up and retreated into the dry. There're still some kids playing around, and a few shifty-looking teenagers startle from a doorway as we pass, running off into the rain with dramatic splashes like hunted animals. Probably a drug deal—loser kids fed up with their cushy but boring existences.

The constant noise of the rainfall steeps everything in a fuzzy-gray layer of unreality, and time stretches out and drags. The muffled splashes of our own footsteps create a bizarre counterpoint, going on and on until I breathe in time with it. We pass towering buildings, with elaborate sweeping designs now acting as water chutes, causing miniature waterfalls on almost every corner, and I notice

Leaf looks totally bedraggled; having shucked his topcoat before leaving the safe house, he's clad only in a thin, dirty-brown shirt clinging to his body, outlining disproportionately large chest muscles. His hair is slicked over his forehead, and he sporadically scrapes it to one side to clear his vision.

We start to jog, and though I'm in good shape, the streaming water pulls uncomfortably at my feet, forcing me to alter my gait to relieve the pressure on my calf muscles. I hope we won't be out here too long, as the first twinges of a cramp are forming from the unnatural movement.

The street becomes more and more uphill, until it's hard going for all of us, and Leaf ducks into a large doorway, shuffling into the corner to make room. He's gasping like a beached fish, and I collapse against the wall, already exhausted, working to stretch out my sore lower legs, and gritting my teeth against the ache. Shit, we're only, what...maybe halfway? I'm gonna have to start using my power to stop the water pressure if this keeps up, and that'll drain me, fast. I need to eat.

As though he's read my mind, Leaf digs around in his cargo pockets and hauls out a few foil-wrapped bars. "Snack break. This here's hard work. Makes ya wonder about that swimmin' stuff ya hear about sometimes." We all take a bar and unwrap it, grateful for the brief respite. After a few glugs of water and a mournful look at the bleak street, Leaf jerks his head. "Alright then, back to it. I reckon we'll hit the first buildin' in about half an hour." He sounds so morose I elbow him gently and force a grin past my own exhaustion. It's up to me to encourage him.

The last thing we need is Leaf bailing and leaving us to find our own way in this awful weather. We'd probably march right into a patrol or wander around in circles until dawn. C'mon, Leaf. Stick with us. We need you. "Least there's no one on the streets, and the cams probably won't grab us in this mess." As soon as I say it, I wish I hadn't. The idea of the Institute watching us makes it all much worse. Soldiers could be converging on our position right now, and in this weather, I wouldn't know until they were on top of me.

He rolls his eyes at me and pointedly wrings out his fringe, a river of water trickling down his neck, but despite his apparent distress, he sniffs and slides out of the doorway. We reluctantly follow his trudging form back into the downpour.

All the water and lack of visual information are so disorientating I'm taken completely by surprise when a Watch patrol almost runs into us at the crossroads. My throat freezes, mouth dropping open. Nuke, we've got to get off the road. What do we do? So much for being trained soldiers. My radar was so jammed I didn't even know they were coming. But the patrol doesn't even hesitate, just runs right past us as we dither.

I clear my throat, embarrassed and pathetically grateful the soldiers were distracted enough by whatever it is they're hunting, to stamp right past. Abial looks as though she feels about the same way, awkwardly looking around the street as she asks, "Well, we'll see them again in a minute. Is there a different route we can take, Leaf?" There's no answer, and I glance around, my breath catching. He's nowhere in sight. "Leaf?" Abial repeats her call a little louder, worry coloring her tone, and he melts out of the gloom in front of us, looking sheepish. I release the breath that had been caught in my throat, strangling me, and try to quash the panic threatening to swamp me.

"Yep. Sorry. Automatic response." He points at the retreating Watch patrol. "Soldiers make me hide." He grins lopsidedly, and I go to pat him on the shoulder, surprised by how relieved I am now he's back. He shifts sideways, avoiding the contact, though, and I drop my hand after an awkward moment, pursing my lips, making a mental note— apparently he doesn't like to be touched.

"Yeah, all right. Not a fighter, we got it. Anyway, alternate route?" My tone is gruffer than I mean it to be.

"Hold it!" An authoritative voice suddenly calls from close behind us, and startled, we spin around. Shit, another soldier. Right when I thought we'd gotten away.

I process several things at once. Leaf is gone again, as though by magic, and there's no sign of him, though it should be impossible we wouldn't have at least heard him splash away. Abial is poised with her hands up, ready to fight. Not the reaction of an innocent civilian, I curse internally. Then another piece of information registers. The soldier who's standing only a couple of meters away from us is, somehow, Gav Belias.

He has his Zap up, pointing at us. I can barely see him in the torrential downpour, but the way he holds his body is unmistakable after the time I spent looking/not looking at him on the tube. Oh, nuke. We're screwed. Does he have backup? I squint through the rain, torn between action and inaction. I could put him down now, hard, but if he's got a team with him and someone radios there're telekinetics in town, the Institute will be on us in minutes.

My mind runs through possibilities, even as I watch him, waiting for a movement, hoping for something to change. It's as though inertia has settled into my muscles, freezing my usually lightning-quick reactions. Fear has its fist around my spine, and I can't force myself to move.

"What are you doing? All Citizens were cleared from this area. Never mind. Put your hands up. You can answer my questions at the Watchhouse." His tone is firm, hands steady, and suddenly another soldier is blurrily visible through the rain behind him.

Feeling Abial questing out with her power shocks me into doing the same, and I waft out mental feelers, looking for information and preparing to attack or defend. I know the other soldiers will also have Zaps. If we get shot from this close, even with the vests, our insides will be minced. Thankfully, my scan lets me know there're only the two of them in immediate range. Not a full patrol. Either they're catching up or scouting ahead. If we take them down simultaneously, they might not get a chance to warn the rest of their pack.

Then more information comes to me: the second man doesn't have any Talent worth mentioning, but Gav Belias, hero of the City Watch, flinches slightly at my mental touch, implying he has some reading ability, at least. He's almost certainly not a telekinetic—he wouldn't be in the Watch if he was—but if he can read, even at a low level, it might account for his brilliant tactical decisions and incredible reaction speed. It's not hard to react fast when you know what's gonna happen before it does.

I catch his intention to shoot and react automatically, thrusting my hand out in a psionic attack at the same moment he fires his Zap. The energy blast from the gun smashes into my surge of power. The noise crashes into my eardrums at the same time the punch of the weapon hits me in the sternum, but my telekinetic push outward, combined with the shock armor, do their jobs. I'm not knocked over, anyway, and there's no time to catalog injuries now.

I send power toward him and twist his arm up before he realizes what's happening, freezing his finger on the trigger so he can't fire again. Even if he doesn't hit me, the sound will bring others. Out of the corner of my eye, I see Abial physically grappling with the second soldier, and in my moment of distraction, Gav Belias pulls a knife with his left hand. Idiot! I scream at myself. Immobilization should have been my first call, but I was flustered and winded and only grabbed his gun hand. He throws so fast it's chain lightning, the knife flying suddenly through the air, and I can't move quickly enough.

I throw more power out, desperate, but it's too slow, and my telekinetic block misses the spinning blade. Fire slices into my cheek as I surge forward, Talent-slamming Gav against the wall behind him with the force of fury, fear, and pain. He crumples like a rag doll, and I look to Abial, frantic. I'm breathing too fast, on the verge of hyperventilating, and I can't remember my training. What should I do? Hot blood is streaming down my cheek. I taste the iron. No, no, no. It can't all go to shit this fast.

I clap a hand to my face and move toward my partner, but Abial already has the man, unconscious, in her arms, dragging him to a smaller road. Shaken and shaking, I jog back to the still form of Gav Belias and slide terror-numb hands under his armpits. I've dragged him almost halfway to the place Abial has chosen to stash the soldiers before I look at him and see the huge depression in the back of his skull. Time slows. Dead. I killed him. I didn't mean to, I just... I just had to make him stop. A small cry escapes my throat, and I run the rest of the way, using telekinesis to take the man...the body with me. Abial hauls me into the alley, and we wait, breathless, for drawn-out minutes, my hand clasped against my face, ignoring the pain from the large cut as I try to stem the flow of blood. It'sforever before Leaf sidles up to us. When he arrives, we tie the unconscious man up and leave him and the body of Gav Belias, hero, on a handy low roof, stoically hauling them up in silence. I remember the story of him running into a burning building saving four slum kids who "weren't supposed to be there."

I determinedly shove down the choking sensation in my chest. Jue is gonna kill me. Why'd I hit him so hard? I didn't have to hit him so *hard*. I have to stop thinking about it, have to focus. Abial gently takes my chin, shaking me out of the moment as she inspects the knife wound. Her fingers feel as though they're burning my skin, like they'll leave prints behind.

She sucks air through her teeth and shrugs. "Well, it's hard to tell how bad it is in the rain, but you definitely need gluing. You're bleeding a lot. Hold still and be quiet." The brutal tone is at odds with her light touch, and I miss the distraction of the contact when she lifts her hand away to find the liquid sutures. The small tube is fiddly, and warm blood puddles inside the neck of my body armor before Abial gets the lid off. I tilt my head back, balling my hands into fists. This isn't my first time being stuck back together, but it might be the worst. I can't see, and it feels horribly as if my cheek's been laid open to the bone, unnervingly close to my eye.

The glue burns as though I'm being cut all over again in slow motion as Abial fills the wound with it, pressing hard fingers around the damaged flesh to ensure it seals properly. The fire only lasts for a few moments, though I have nail marks in my palms by the time Abial nods, satisfied the bleeding has stopped. Knee-jerk reactions are gonna get people killed. They told me. Kion was right. The Watch are mostly good guys. Misled, sure, but...not bad. And I killed him. My brain keeps sticking on the way he crumpled when he hit the wall, the lack of light in his eyes as he lolled in my arms.

Leaf shuffles awkwardly, avoiding my eyes. "So, this'd be the way, if we're still goin'?" I glower and pad my fingers over the freshly sealed, but still painful cut, much to Abial's clear disapproval.

"Yeah, we're still going. It's a scratch." Nothing's gonna stop me from finishing this mission. I look up at the roof where we stowed Gav again. His face was so slack and pale... But then I clench my jaw. Deal with it later. Put it away. "Time to go." Without further ado, we lope down an adjoining street, and Leaf pulls us to a halt before we rejoin the main road.

"Looky." He points upward at a towering six-story building. "That's the badger."

Abial furrows her eyebrows in confusion. "What's a badger?" I elbow her and jerk my chin at the building.

"First target, right? So this could be the place? Guess we should figure out where the boys in black've gone. And get in there. Run a sweep." Determinedly not dealing with the earlier events, I put the mission in my sights, my senses tingling with the adrenaline pumping through my system. I'm ready to move. To get it over with.

"Out of interest, why do ya think yer target'll stay put, instead've running like he's been doin'? I mean, if he's even 'ere," Leaf inquires, scraping his hair off his face with difficulty and plastering it firmly to one side.

Focus. The team needs my head in the game. I manage a half grin and lift a shoulder. "Do we look like the bad guys? Look how cute we are! Would he run from us?" I flutter my eyelashes at him, placing my hand under my chin and pretending to be a city girl mooning after a handsome boy. He snorts.

"Yeah, sounds probable, especially with blood all over yer face. Ya reckon ya can find the next buildin' if he's not 'ere, or shall I stick around?" He obviously doesn't want to stay, uncomfortable with the turn of events and the idea of waiting where the Watch could pick him up. I roll my eyes and shake my head slightly. He's done more than enough. He's not a security blanket.

I'm a soldier, he's not. Do your job. Let him go. "Nah, you bounce. We'll see you outside. You've done your bit. Now go sort out some explosions. I'll comm you when we're clear. Good luck." I'm pleased that I sound strong, not desperate for him to disagree with me, to stay for a little longer and help carry the weight crushing me.

Leaf smiles slowly—a broad smile showing his crooked teeth. "Nah, luck's for suckers. I've got skills on my side. Be seein' yah." And he disappears into the murk without seeming to move.

Abial shivers. "See. Creeeeeepy. I wish I could do that, though." I shrug, puffing out a lungful of air and wiping water off my forehead. In this rain, it's a losing battle, and the water is starting to drive me nuts. It's dulling my instincts.

I look at the space Leaf vanished into for a long moment. I hope he keeps his word. We'll need a diversion if we hope to get clear. "Folks in the townships'd say he's touched. No one should move so sneaky." Cracking my neck from side to side, I adjust the pack on my back and check I can still reach my altered Zap without exposing it. Not that it matters if anyone sees the weapon, at this point. I bet I look a sight. "D'ya reckon Zaps are waterproof?" I carry on, speaking without waiting for a reply. "Right, so, set to low, yeah? We don't want a boom loud enough to put the Watch onto us. Actually, we should keep them holstered, unless we're about to die, thinking about it. Stick to smashing people's heads against the walls?" Just get on with it. I know I'm talking too much—more than necessary—but I can't stop myself.

Abial's lip curls sardonically. "Yeah, you're good at that." It sounds like an accusation, and I flinch at her tone, tugging my shirt straight and bouncing in place for a moment to check my shoes. They squelch.

"So're you. We're a good team." *We were a good team. Maybe not anymore.* I didn't mean to project, but I must have. To my surprise, Abial looks awkward, hunching her shoulders like a child who's been caught doing something naughty.

She pauses for a moment and then nods. "Yeah. I guess we are. Look. I'm sorry about your test. It wasn't scorch."

I blink, taken aback, then quirk my mouth, reminded of my injury when it stings. "Nah, not okay at all. We can figure it out after this job. I'm bored of being wet. Let's go." Besides, I murdered a man today. There are bigger things on our plate right now. I almost don't care anymore; the reality of the mission has made me feel as if all the friendships, tests, cheating, and passing in the world don't matter a jot. I just want to get in and find out what the Institute's after. I hope it's worth killing for.

Abial accepts the dismissal with a frown and glances around, pulling out the datapad and running a program displaying the blueprints of the building. "Six stories are a lot to search. One at each side and work our way up?"

"It's the best way to cover the ground. Keep our powers in tight but use them to scan, I reckon. The Watch isn't here, anyway. They must have been headed somewhere else." So this might well be a dead end. Only one way to find out. With a last glance at the building and each other, we inch toward the main street. At least it's dark, the strip lighting on the roof edges only illuminating a small section of rain; as long as we avoid them, we'll be basically invisible. On my mental count of three, we waft our powers out and sprint toward the waiting building.

The lashing rain drives into my eyes, even with my head lowered, and I rely on tendrils of power to steady my feet and read my surroundings. I duck into the niche between the corner of the building and the next, glancing around to make sure I've drawn no attention to myself. On the opposite side, I sense Abial doing the same. With the ease of practice, we link our Talents together, meshing our awareness in a way to allow us to keep track of each other. We're both being careful to keep it surface thought only, denying the possibility of a deeper connection, but it still feels better, feels good to be back on the same page. We push our power into the building. It only takes a few minutes for us to agree it's empty, with no signs of movement.

Of course, the target could be shielded and sitting perfectly still, and therefore come across as invisible. *It would be useful if powers could be used to read heat*, I muse, passing the thought to Abial, who sends a silent agreement back. I make a mental note to hand the thought over to one of the geeks back at base. Frustrated, we trot around the building, and Abial checks her datapad for the next location. This journey is equally as hellish as the first but only takes ten minutes.

Then we see two Watch patrols, the second of which is waiting outside the next building on our hit list. There's also an elec-car with a cadaverous teenage boy flanked by two granite-faced soldiers in the center of the group of Watch personnel. The boy's head is shaved and marked with distinctive triangular tattoos that cause bile to rise up in my throat. Institute. Reader.

Slamming our powers down with the speed of terror, we dive into the shadow of an alleyway and press ourselves against the wall, breathing harshly through our noses and not daring to move. I relax slightly after a few moments pass with no alert from the patrol and slide a wet and chilled hand toward Abial, who takes it. It's not for comfort, but I take it from the connection anyway. Now we can communicate mind to mind while remaining shielded from the Institute Reader, by connecting our powers directly, skin to skin, shield to shield. *Nuke.* My mental curse is so vehement Abial flinches before responding.

*Plan? Do you think the target's here? Should we check the other buildings, just in case?*

My answer is full of growling rage. *What if whoever they're looking for gets caught and dies while we're off somewhere else? We gotta go in. We can't scan, the slave'll catch us. Do you think...?* I try not to scrunch my face in distress, to avoid tugging painfully at the three-inch gash marring my cheek.

Abial knows exactly what I'm thinking and responds immediately. *We can't break the boy out. We're stealth, remember? We get our target, and we're outta here. How long do we have?* She's matter-of-fact. To her, the Reader's nothing but another enemy. To me, though, he's Damon. They're all Damon, every single kid taken and used for their skills. This skinny teenager is someone's child, someone's sibling. I'm wrung out, exhausted after too much, too soon. The tears are stinging my eyes, so I let them fall, knowing they'll get lost in the rain. Through the blur, I notice Abial tapping frantically on her datapad. The screen is dark, I realize, right as Abial confirms with a thoughtform. *Nuke, my tech's down. You?*

Distracted, I frown and tap on my wrist unit, then groan internally. *Yep, me too. They must have thrown a pulse at the place. We've got, what, about three hours to get to the Wall? If we can't comm Leaf, we have to be there in time and pray he remembers. We don't have any time to waste.*

We both lean for a moment, minds racing, and then Abial groans internally. *We need a plan! Come on, Tactics! This is your thing, right?*

I shake myself and nod grimly. This is what I'm here for. Plans on the fly. Creative thinking. Well, a distraction to move us away from here would be good. *How far's the next building? I wish we could raise Leaf and ask him to lob a grenade through the window or whatever. A decent boom at one of the suspected locations should move them along; they'd have to assume something big was happening and head that way, leaving this place unmanned, at least for a few minutes.*

Abial snorts silently and purses her lips in thought. *They're getting ready to go in. One of us should do it. The next building's only a few blocks away.* She clenches her jaw, flaring her nostrils and meeting my eyes with a serious expression as she lays the offer out. *Give me a grenade, I'll go. All I've got to do is get there, throw it in, and get out of the area. If I sprint, I can be there in a minute. Hurry. I'll head back here to meet you as soon as I can. If I'm not back in fifteen minutes, head for the Wall.*

The thing about mind-to-mind communication is that emotion and feeling are always layered through the words, even when you're trying to hide it. I feel Abial's urgency and determination, calculate the odds of us getting to the building with a Reader on-site—nil—and growl under my breath. I can't see a way around it. We need to get attention away from the place. Abial's a faster runner, with those stupid long legs. I haul my flat pack to the front and dig through it, then hand Abial two egg-sized grenades and an extra power pack for her Zap. *Good luck.*

If Abial doesn't get back, doesn't meet up with me, there's no way I can lift someone over the Wall by myself. If I'm unfathomably lucky, the target might have enough telekinesis to help, but even then, without practice and training...the odds aren't good. More likely, I'll have to terminate the target, hide out in the City. Hope Leaf finds me, or I can get through the Wall into the slums on my fake ID. Not great options, but it's all we have unless we abort the mission now. Which we won't. Neither of us considers that an option.

All of this, Abial knows. We're linked together. She knows exactly how I feel the same as I know how she feels. How darkly, ceaselessly angry she still is with me. There's no need or time to say anything else. Abial pockets the weapons, grins almost invisibly in the darkness, and she's gone.

A nauseous feeling has settled in my stomach, and I can't shake the thought that I'm sending Abial off to die. Biting the inside of my uninjured cheek, I remind myself why we're here, then edge to the end of the wall and peek out, relying on the gloom to hide me. The soldiers are slowly getting into a skirmish line, obviously ready to bust through the doors. I brace, wondering whether Abial has found trouble, or if she's on her way to the other building. If she's already dead. And then, suddenly, a muffled boom breaks through the heavy sound of rain.

The soldiers immediately start backing away from the building and forming a cordon around their treasured cargo—the boy in the car. Orders are hand-signed from soldier to soldier as the unit reorganizes itself and bolts at a fast clip toward the explosion, elec-car whirring around and keeping pace easily. All right! Something finally goes our way. Now stay out of sight, Abial. Don't die. Don't you dare leave me. Abial's too far away to actually receive the message even if I was sending it out, but it makes me feel better to wish the thought, anyway. I wait until I can't make out the soldiers anymore, and then slink over to the building they were watching. This is it—they must think their quarry is here, or they wouldn't have been preparing the way they were. The Reader would have told them for certain someone was in this building, and that's all I really need to know. I have to get in there. I'm too scared of the Reader to use my powers, so I huddle in the doorway and start hacking open the electronic lock with my wrist unit.

# Part Six

# Sam

AN INDETERMINATE PERIOD of time later, after eight buildings' worth of power tapping and squirreling information away to where I can access it for the final stage of my plan, my hidey-hole is surrounded by soldiers, and I'm at the end of my tether. I started hallucinating from exhaustion a while ago—spiders crawling across my vision and people behind me who aren't there when I spin around.

That's why, when the soldiers suddenly abandon their intention of breaking in the main door to the office building I'm cowering in, I assume I'm imagining things. The bombs pressed all around the ceiling of the room send out comforting pulses of "I'm ready, I'm ready," and I wonder if I'm ready to die as I wait for the inevitable incursion. Should I set them off now? Is there any point in killing soldiers?

What I don't expect to see, on the security cam by the front door, is a disheveled teenage girl. Wild, curly hair is plastered to her skull from the weird rainstorm, which started...sometime. I don't even know how long I've been running. Forever? Days, at least. But the storm rages on—I see the rain hitting the street behind this stranger.

She rummages in her bag, glaring at the lock and then looking down the street after the soldiers. Then straight up at the camera. She has freakishly light eyes, large and luminous in the darkness, and when they connect with mine through the screen, inside my chest, I feel a dragging and catching sensation. Friend.

I send a thoughtform to the door she's hacking, so it clicks open under her hands. She starts in surprise, and I hunch over the datapad. As soon as our eye contact is severed, my mouth drops open. Why did I do that? Why did I unlock the door? I follow her progress by switching cam views until she gets to the room I'm in, then shut the datapad into near blackness with the twitch of a finger.

Getting to my feet, I wait in the darkness, breathing thin and light, terror clasping a tight fist around my esophagus. This could be a trap—she has to be a Psionic, tricking me into opening the door. And Psionics work for the Institute. Except...well, me. I guess. Could she really be a friend? With the whole military after me, the idea of not being alone makes my heart stutter in hope.

The girl bumps into a few things, and I sense a Zap in her hands, but I think she's too young to be Watch. She looks fifteen or so, though I guess you can't really tell with girls, a lot of the time. But why is she here by herself?

My stomach clenches in fear when she aims the nose of the weapon at me, and suddenly she calls out, "I'm warning you. I've got a Zap pointed right at you. I'm not with the Watch."

Duh, I think, exhaustion and tension warring in me. Half of me is about to pass out, while the other half wants to scream and run at her, take her Zap, and use it to splatter my brains all over the wall so I don't have to feel this way anymore. Then an idea strikes me, and I narrow my eyes, hijacking the intercom system in the room and sending a question through it using splices of voice clips from vids.

"How about the people who want to open up my skull and play pat-a-cake with my brain? You with them?" The robot-sounding words make her jump, and she spins around, pointing the Zap at the speaker before figuring out what happened.

"No, not with them either. Not really into unrequited brain surgery." Something deep and dark in her voice hits me right in the chest, and suddenly I believe her. I trust her, although I'm struggling to figure out why.

Hatred, I realize. There's hatred in her voice, and that's enough for me. I turn the brightness on my datapad back up, illuminating the room, and she twists, Zap up and pointed at my chest. My Adam's apple catches in my throat as I gulp at the action. I'm so sick of being scared. If this girl can offer me a way out, I'll take it.

"Unrequited brain surgery is the worst kind of surgery. I should know. Hi, I'm Sam. Who're you?" Her face is bloody and swollen, an angry cut peaking across her cheek in an ugly line and marring her pale cheek. She's pretty, in a feral sort of way. "What happened to your face?"

She ignores my question. "My name's Serena. I'm here to get you out. Are you hurt?" Her voice is kind, and the last person I spoke to who cared about me was my mother.

The weight of loss hits me again, and my knees suddenly give way, sending me crumpling to the floor, tears welling in my eyes. But I refuse to cry within the first few minutes of meeting someone, so I focus on her questions. "Not really. I'm pretty hungry, though. I haven't eaten in two days."

The datapad suddenly alerts me there's a new file out with my name on it. It's biometrics—they've finally released my status to the public, to try to enlist the populace in their search. I glower and dive in to change the details—confuse the issue as much as possible. I switch the picture of me out for a kid who died last year. Hopefully, the conflicting information will slow them up a bit. Give me more time. Before they inevitably catch me.

The girl, Serena, clears her throat, making me jump. "You need help?" Meeting her gaze swamps me in another wave of unexpected trust. She looks strong, although she's three inches shorter than me, and there's something about the set of her jaw and the laser clarity of her eyes implies she doesn't take any shit.

The look makes me want to show her I'm not only someone who needs saving. I mean, I am someone who needs saving right now, but I have stuff going for me as well. So I spin the datapad so she can see what I'm working with— Institute files, data, maps, protocol, communications, and folder after folder of classified material.

Her mouth falls open, framing words that don't make it clear of her tongue, and a little curl of pride warms my stomach. She might be tough—a soldier, a warrior—but I've surprised her.

Finally, she manages to choke words out. "Nuke, you're in their systems! Comms, maps, protocol... How in the name of freedom did you get this?"

The tone of her voice and the way she says "their" cements it for me. I look up at the pinlights flashing around the room. "Well, I guess you really aren't with them, then. I should probably disable the bombs."

"What bombs? Nuke, who are you?" She scans the room, wide-eyed and even paler than she was before. I don't answer immediately, but shut off the fuses on the bombs, my talent fizzing and popping uncomfortably in my mind in its weakened state. The green lights disappear into dormancy, and I turn back to her.

"I told you, I'm Sam. Can you get me out of the City? I can pay. Whatever you want. A million credits." I stagger upright, using the wall as a convenient leaning post, muscles shaking and protesting. I'm dead on my feet and can't run by myself anymore. My best hope of survival is escaping the City limits, and this is the only person I've met who seems to be an ally, so I make the decision to trust her pretty easily.

After all, I've been a dead boy for days, just walking around. If she can help me, maybe everything isn't lost. If I finish what I'm doing, find a secure place to upload everything and put it on every screen in the country... Well. That would be a thing worth doing. Worth dying for, even.

"Uh...muh...mih... A million credits?" She sounds like she might be about to fall over. "Nuke me now. You're rad touched. Mad."

A weak grin surprises me; the look on her face is hilarious, and I'm punch-drunk, giddy from exhaustion and fear. I shrug self-deprecatingly before replying. "Nah, just good with computers. Steal a bit here, steal a bit there... If you steal half a credit from everyone in the system, the computers simply round up and no one's the wiser. S'pretty useful. Do you have any food?"

The burning, hollow hunger in my guts is a demanding beast refusing to be ignored, not if I expect to move anywhere without passing out. I'm as weak as a day-old hamster. Across the room, the soldier girl eyes me, and there's a tickle in my head. Blinking in surprise, I get confirmation for what I'd only guessed before.

She's a telepath, like me, but not like me at all.

She's rummaging in my head, looking for information about who I am and what I've done. Fair enough. I relax, willing myself not to respond, and after a moment she withdraws, apparently satisfied. She smiles at me and waits. I think she's expecting me to do the same, but I don't know how, or if I'm even capable, so I think about looking in her head, as though it will help. It must work, because she nods and digs through her bag, walking toward me. She finds energy bars and a water flask, and I reach out and grab them, frustrated beyond comprehension as I fumble clumsily with the wrapping.

Then she helps me open them, and I fall on the food ravenously, unable to repress the desperate noise bursting out of my throat as the smell reaches my nostrils. She looks away as I eat, and finally, after three bars and several sloppy gulps of water to wash down the dry paste, the gnawing pain in my gut subsides enough to let me focus. I scrub my hand through my hair, realizing belatedly the bandage covering my surgery site has dropped off sometime in the last few days.

Great, the wound'll be crawling with bacteria.

Sniffing, I figure I can deal with it later, if I survive. Which for the first time is a faint possibility. Hope is a minute flicker in my chest against the ice of despair, but it's better than nothing.

"Way out of the City? Yes? No? Maybe?"

She grins confidently, looking every inch the professional, and I'm filled with a sense of relief. Clearly, she knows exactly what she's doing. I'm sick of reacting frantically, trying to stay one step ahead, so her certainty is reassuring.

"Uh. Yeah. My buddy's putting together a distraction for us. Gotta pick up my partner real quick, but then we can bounce outta here. Get to nicer weather, maybe." She smiles at me and gestures around the room. "I'll clean your prints off, sit for a minute."

"Nah, it's okay. I'll change 'em for someone else's later." She looks taken aback, and I shrug, waggling the datapad at her. "Really good with computers."

A confused look paints her face, but she shrugs. "If you're sure. Right, let's go find Abial."

Abial. Another soldier to protect me. I store the name away for future reference and take a few stuttering steps toward her, thrusting the datapad out before I change my mind. This will be safer with her. If anyone has a shot at getting out of the City alive, it's sure as shit not me, and this girl can use what's on here already. The information I've gathered. I might die, but I'll leave a legacy behind.

I think she might have dust in her eye, because she scrubs at it furiously when she takes the datapad, and then turns with a determined air, jogging to the stairs and motioning me to follow. I do so in silence, happy to let her deal with everything for a while. When we get outside, we huddle against a wall, clearly waiting for some reason.

I jump when an angry-looking girl with a broad Asian face, high cheekbones, and rage in her dark eyes slips out of the darkness, but Serena looks relieved for a moment. It must be her partner. Serena rapidly fills the new girl in while the rain shields us in our fairly lousy hiding spot; then she turns to me and asks me to turn the fuses back on and set off the bombs in the building.

I do it. We wait a few moments until it collapses with a roar, and then we're on our way.

The journey is a numbing, soul-destroying nightmare of wet and cold. I'm shaking so hard I can barely focus enough to loop the camera feeds, but the girls take it in turns to half carry me as I basically shut my eyes and try not to trip over my own feet. I don't know how long we've walked, but eventually my knees refuse to go any farther, and I slip out of their grasp, sliding to the flooded ground. They drag me to a door, then take so long opening it I rouse myself enough to slip the lock, even though I don't know what's waiting on the other side.

There's a pause before they bundle me inside, and I wonder if they've ever seen a technopath before. If they have any idea what I can do. It doesn't seem like they do.

Once we're in the house, they have some sort of discussion about an EMP—electromagnetic pulse—that destroyed their tech, and my fuzzy brain tries to tell me something. Oh. Dredging up the energy to speak is difficult, but I manage it.

"Actually, I did it. The EMP thing. Your tech will be fine now. Try it."

For a moment, I think Serena is going to hit me, and it dawns on me that by screwing all the tech in the area, I separated them from their support system and communications. Nuke. She swallows her anger, to my relief, and I try to look apologetic.

Then a fire is conjured out of somewhere, and I curl myself up as close as I can to let the heat seep into my frozen bones. The girls murmur to each other while I drift into a sort of half sleep, their soft chatter soothing me into relaxing for the first time in what feels like years. My brain is glazed over from too much stress and shock and panic, dazed to the point of incomprehension.

But then a hand shakes my shoulder, rousing me from my dreamy state, and I jump a little. Serena is peering at me. "Can you run for a minute, cowboy?"

No. I wonder if they'll leave me or kill me if I can't. Making a face, I wrap my arms across my body and think about my mother. She'd want me to keep going. "I can try." After all, the soldiers are still coming, still combing the City for me. They must have discovered the building I blew up by now. And our trail. The girls can probably fight, but I can't. I've used every trick I've ever thought of, and more, in moments of pure desperation, and still I don't know how I made it this far. Just because there's three of us won't stop me from being the first to die. And there's no guarantee they won't go on without me if there's trouble. I'm slowing them down, putting them in danger, and now they have the datapad, they could well decide to cut their losses and go on alone. I sniff nervously and get to my feet. My legs are shaking, but I can walk. Barely.

# Serena

IT HAS TO be good enough. We don't have any time to waste. Soldiers should be headed for City Hall, but it won't take them long to realize it's an isolated incident. They might even realize it's a distraction. Abial holds a hand up, signaling us to wait as she peers into the darkness. A moment passes, and then we slip from the relative safety of the building and streak toward the Wall. My feet slip and slide on the soaked solar panels, and I rely on my power to keep my footing, thrusting minute pegs of it into the floor to anchor me as I sprint.

Sam is faring badly, feet slithering out from under him, basically skating as I drag him along. When I let him go, he coasts for a moment and crashes to a halt against the Wall, collapsing into a heap. There's no time to care for him; I have to be ready; the timing has to be perfect. Abial has dropped behind, slowing her steps to giant, forceful stomps as I skid to a halt, telekinetically mooring myself to the floor. I cast power around my calves and deep into the ground to brace myself as I twist around.

The move hurts as if I've run straight into a brick wall, and even my telepathically reinforced joints screech in angry protest. But Abial is already stepping up and into my waiting hands, the leap fitting into her rhythmic strides so well I can't help the grin spreading over my face as I thrust upward. Just like we've practiced. Abial's slipper is soaked through, clammy and rubbery for the brief moment it presses on my palm before she's catapulted into the air with inhuman force.

She throws her power out and down at the same time as I push, and we force our Talents to work against one another. Abial flies high into the air, toward the far-away top of the Wall. When she begins to slow, I shove again, ramming power up toward my partner, and Abial's now-distant body is jerked upward again. I hold my breath for a moment, knowing the strain is visible on my face, but I can't stop. Abial's out of sight, blocked from view by the darkness and the rain, and I can't relax until it's clear my partner has landed. If she comes plummeting back toward the ground, we've failed. And if that happens, Sam and I will be stuck on this side of the Wall, without an ally.

A long minute passes, and nothing moves in the murk around me. Finally, I blow out my breath. She must have made it, or she'd be falling by now. Thank nuke for years of practice. Now to get the kid over and myself. Piece of cake. I try to swallow, my mouth suddenly dry. It comes out as a gulp. Sam looks as though he's been poleaxed, his mouth hanging open even as he huddles against the imposing hugeness of the Wall.

I grin weakly, completely unable to manage anything more encouraging, and cup my hands, lacing my fingers together. I can't even imagine facing this jump without telekinesis to fall back on. "Your turn."

He sidles away, spine pressed tightly against the edifice behind him. "No, no, no. My power doesn't work that way. I'll fall." His voice trembles, sounding as if he's close to tears, and his eyes are huge, the whites clearly visible, rimming the irises.

For a second, I have to fight the overwhelming urge to slap him, the hours of tension pushing me to the boiling point. I shove the feeling away determinedly, getting ahold of myself. "If you stay here, you die. If you jump, Abial will catch you. When we came up with this plan, we didn't know you had any gift at all, so believe me, we could do this with a chair if we had to. And you, at least, have hands. So you'll be able to grab her. She's waiting on the top, okay? We've done this before." It's a white lie. I try to look encouraging, but it's probably ruined by the nervous glances around us, eyes flicking away from his in order to check our surroundings.

"Look, we've gotta do this. You do it now, or I go and leave you here. Your call." I'm not sure I actually would, but if it came to it, I'm not convinced we'd be able to get out any other way, anyhow. It's this or nothing. There's no chance I'm strong enough to jump with myself and Sam. As it is, this will be the highest jump I've ever made, and the second person always has a much harder job with no one to boost them. I'm going to have to throw telekinetic "arms" up, Talent jump as high as I can, and hope Abial grabs me in time. At least if I fall, I should have enough gift left to catch myself. Maybe. But none of that will be any good if Sam won't go first.

A choking sound forces its way out of his throat, but he presses bloodless lips together and manages a small nod. "Okay. Okay. You swear you won't drop me?"

"On my life." I'm deadly serious, and he closes his eyes for a long second before steadying himself on the Wall, hand splayed, and lifting his leg. I cup my hands and he wedges his foot into them. "I'm gonna throw you on three. Abial's waiting, and she's gonna pull you the rest of the way. Stretch your arms up as far as you can. If you miss, I'll catch you.

Our powers do work this way, okay? Trust us." Trust us. This is the only plan we have.

"Okay." His face looks carved from marble, and he swallows jerkily. "I guess I'd rather splat on the ground than end up back on a surgery gurney, anyway." He touches his head, lost in a memory. Poor kid, how long did they have him? How did he get away? I open my mouth, about to ask, and then remember our situation. There'll be time for questions later, if we all survive.

I crouch down farther, squeezing his foot. "Ready? One, two, three." On the word "three," I throw him upward with all my might—physical and telekinetic. He flies fast, his arms flailing above him as if he hopes he'll be able to grab something now. But the Wall is smooth and impenetrable, with nothing to hook fingers onto. Unclimbable. If he touches it, all he'll succeed in doing is slowing his crazy flight. I'm staring at his squirming body so intently I don't even blink with the rain pattering against my eyes.

From behind me, a yell breaks the ominous non-silence of the water hitting the ground. I pull my power up into a shield, tensing in anticipation of shots tearing my protections to shreds. I can't jump until I know Abial has him. I crouch on the balls of my feet, ready to run from the soldiers who must be coming. The seconds last forever. My back waits and waits for the thumping impact of Zap shots. Will I have any warning? Or will they tear me apart before I even know they've shot me? Finally, Sam slows, clearly about to reverse direction. No shots from behind yet. I'm itching to look, but I can't.

Instead, I prepare for him to fall—for the shattering, body-smashing fall I'll have to keep from ending in blood. And then, right when he must be about to plunge back to the ground, he jerks a little and is suddenly yanked skyward, out of sight. I look around, scanning for the soldiers. But there's no one there. Either I imagined the shout, or it wasn't focused on me. Thank Google.

I swallow, and my gaze flies back up at the imposing construction. Forty-eight meters of solid white, slick and running with water. It's huge. I could swear it's never been this big before, but Abial and Sam are already at the top, and I have to try. A small, ugly part of me thinks if I don't, I might be able to get out of the City through the gates and meet them in the slums. For a moment, I consider it. But no, we're safer together, and I'd never forgive myself if they got caught while I was swanning around, lying to border guards with a fake ID. Who knows if I'd make it through, anyway? Sniffing and taking a second to swipe tendrils of wet hair from my face, I relax, gathering power.

I envision my body, as I've practiced so many times—the structure making the very shape of me. Threads of muscle and cords of sinew, bands of bone and cartilage. Pipes full of blood. I fill the tensed fibers of thighs and calves with power, packing it in, envisioning the sparkling turquoise light building up and up and up, every cell of me stuffed with energy. Ready for use. It's the Serena Slam, but through my feet, combined with an outward thrust of power. No problem. Just as I think that, another shout echoes from behind me. No mistaking it, this one is close. I chance a look, and to my horror, see eight or nine shapes rushing toward me out of the misty rain. No time.

Turning my attention back to the Wall, inches from my body, I coil and leap, ignoring my screaming knees, driving Talent out of my soles with such fierceness that the wet slippers are left behind, a silent witness to my jump. The wind whistles in my ears, and a shot fires below me, hitting the Wall and sending a tremor through the air. But it's like they don't see where I am—can't figure out where I could possibly have gone—because no more shots follow. Nothing hits my shields to send me back down in a wet heap of shredded muscle.

In front of me, the Wall is everything—it's all I see in every direction but below. I don't dare to look down. The power of my initial push is already waning, and I'm slowing, enough that I can see a horizontal hairline between the blocks forming the protection of the City. Desperate, I look up, hurling my Talent above me, searching for Abial's. For a moment I hang motionless, unsupported in the air, my stomach threatening to reject its contents, leaning forward so bare toes and cold hands press against the Wall in a last-ditch effort to somehow catch myself. Don't look down. My feet start to slip, I'm falling... Abial's power suddenly roars around me, spreading through the air and finally getting a grip on my physical body.

Then I'm pulling myself upward even as Abial hauls me, all grace gone in desperation, our combined gifts dragging me painfully, slowly along the icy surface, until I'm bellying over the rim of the Wall. Rolling away from the edge, I gasp, face up and limbs splayed. From above, Abial laughs at me; not cruelly, but with clear disbelief and joy. There's happiness in her face I haven't seen for months. There must have been a moment there when she also believed I wasn't gonna make it.

The sound is faint in the pervasive, dampening sound of the rain, and when I look past my partner, Sam is sitting, looking out over the City, his hands pressed tightly against the Wall's surface, as if he's afraid he'll slide right over the side. I follow his eye line and gasp. The view is somehow beautiful—the tips of the buildings scarcely visible, and the Wall smearing around, a huge road in the sky.

In the distance, a lightning strike illuminates the skies and silhouettes Abial against the City skyline, jagged building tops and sweeping curves dwarfing her lithe frame. She squats. "Holy shit." *I didn't think you were gonna make it.* I hear "I'm glad you made it" between the lines and the tightness, present in my chest for months, loosens a fraction.

"Yeah." *Me too. Thanks. There were soldiers. Keep an eye out. I'll get Sam down. In a minute...*

Abial nods in acquiescence, and I watch, relieved, as she crouches on the City side of the Wall, alert and scanning the horizon for threats. Lying there, I make out an orange glow, far in the distance. Leaf's explosion. Must be. It looks big. I hope he made it away, made it out of there before being overrun by the military response. It takes a few minutes for me to get my breath and courage back, lying there and staring at the black skies.

The sheer enormity of the Wall is exaggerated by the mere fact that we're on top of it. It's wider than a street, and we're far enough from the edges there's no danger of tumbling off. Sam's panting a little, I see, but managing to get under control, and I struggle to my feet, feeling wrung out but knowing there's no time to rest. We're exposed, the wind tugging at our clothes, yanking at the wet fabric and trying to drag me over the side. Added to that is the fact it won't be long before the soldiers below figure out where I must have gone, impossible though it will look to them. Maybe they'll decide I had a grapnel or a zip line. Whatever they use to explain my disappearance away, once they spend a moment checking the nearby streets, they'll send choppers to check the area.

We have to go. Now. I force myself to limp over to Sam, knees feeling twice their normal size, and stand in front of him, unable to crouch, ruffling his hair to get his attention. He blinks, bleary-eyed, and focuses on me. "Almost there, my dude. One scarier bit and we're out. We have a house lined up; we'll be dry, warm. Fed. And then we're taking you back with us to a place where you'll be safe for as long as you want. Okay? Hold on for a little bit longer." My voice sounds remarkably steady. I'm glad it doesn't sound as shaky as my legs are after telekinetically propelling myself farther than anyone I've ever heard of doing.

He gets shakily to his feet with my help, and we edge toward the drop, though he refuses to look over the edge, even as I peer into the swampy darkness below. Abial's still crouching on the far side, watching for threats. Sam slaps himself on the cheek a few times, looks at the angry sky for a moment, and then meets my eyes.

"Let's do it."

"Count to thirty. I'll catch you." I look at him seriously, wait for his nod, and then step off the edge. This way is much easier, but terrifying in a whole new way. I drop like a stone, and it's a roller coaster; it's lying on top of the tube; it's rushing liquid and air; and it's scrunched-tight eyes, with my back scraping painfully down a vertical waterslide and my power thrusting out below me, waiting for contact with the ground...there...so I can push, catch myself with an invisible air cushion, and slow my descent until my bare feet slam into the swampy ground, mud spurting between my bare toes. My knees collapse under the new impact, and I fold slowly to the ground.

Clambering to my feet is one of the hardest things I've ever done. It takes too long. I hastily reach my hands out and take stock of my remaining power. There's enough left for this, thank Google. Sam will be coming any second now... I think I'm ready, but the rush of him hurtling out of the darkness startles me, and I just manage to shove my power at him, slowing his flailing body in the same way I slowed myself.

Suddenly I pause, almost dropping him in a split second of distraction. There's a strange noise in the air that could be distant thunder, but I can't split my attention right now; I need to steady him until he's on the ground. He's skidding madly at an angle, my power pressing him against the Wall as I grit my teeth and grunt with the effort of impeding his sickening rush toward the ground.

After a shaky moment of working hard to keep him safe, he plops into the mud in front of me. He immediately vomits into a puddle and curls up into the fetal position. Meanwhile, the noise I heard is getting louder, whomping in the distance. It's familiar...not the cracking sound of thunder. I grab his shoulder, urging him to his feet as the throbbing sound fills the air and a weird light illuminates the rain above us. I squint through it, looking for Abial, hunting for our connection.

A series of popping sounds break the spell, and I finally connect the light and the noise. Choppers... Zapfire! The soldiers have already figured us out, and reinforcements are here! I crush Sam against the Wall, hiding us in the overshadowing blackness, while pain explodes above me.

The constant, low-level connection to Abial disintegrates. All at once, she's gone, replaced by a howling, dark pit. A connection that's been with me for years is imploding, forcing me to pull away from it lest I'm sucked into madness from the pain. It's reflexive, the same way I'd yank my hand from a hot stove, but the sensation is utterly incomprehensible; I can't connect the feeling to any fact and stare up into the erratically lit night. Looking for my friend.

A helpless keening noise comes out of my throat, while I hold my hands out as if I can make it stop. A black and inconceivable shape is falling, bouncing off the Wall. Once. Twice. I push power out and wrap it around the thing, pulling it away from the Wall, slowing it the way I did for Sam. Something in my chest collapses, a punctured balloon. I lay my burden down gently.

It's Abial, but instead of landing on her feet like a cat, she's horizontal. The puddle she's lying in is reflecting moonlight and looks almost white. Sam starts forward as I slump to my damaged knees, crawling the distance between us. The brown-red mud of soaking slum dust coats me, sticking to hands and legs and elbows, holding me as if it wants to stop me from reaching Abial. It feels as if it takes me an hour to get to her. When I finally, painfully do, I reach out.

My hands are twitching. They're also dirty, caked in grime. I can't help Abial if I'm covered in mud. I choke, hastily rubbing them together and wiping them off on my thighs. Then I delicately set them on Abial's torso, searching for injuries, exactly the way we were taught. I can't feel anything—it's all soft and wet. *Come on, come on. You're okay. I caught you, you're okay. You have to be okay.* I try to make sense of the scene in the stuttering light. Abial is jerking, and my hands are dipped in black, then red. Red.

Abial wheezes, coughing a drop of blood that flies up and then falls onto her cheek, only to be immediately washed away by the rain. Her hair is sticking to her face in a dark sheet, hiding her eyes. I push it back, frantically trying to decide what to do. Abial's pupils are blown wide and impossibly dark, almost obscuring the familiar ring of deep coppery brown. The light cuts again. Sam slumps on his heels, a ghost of a boy in the shadow of the Wall. There's a roaring noise in my ears—no—overhead. I look up, tilting my face against the rain and howl an animal's shout of pain and outrage, bursting out of my chest so fiercely I'm almost shocked I can't see it plunging through the air.

A chopper is banking in the skies, its searchlight twisting. It will be on us in moments. I fumble for my Zap, fingers made of rubber, twisting around the trigger, and haul it out of my soaked pants, but Sam staggers forward, jabbing his hand into my armpit and hauling me up with a reserve of strength I didn't know he had in him. "Bring her. Pick her up. Now. Run." His voice breaks in the middle, but it's firm. Gasping, I obey, sliding my hands under Abial's shoulders and knees, and scooping her up. We stumble forward, the white light of the chopper brushing over the stone behind us, inches away from my heels. I risk a glance back to see a pool of blood-filled water, shockingly lurid against the monochrome surroundings. But Sam twists, dragging my attention away from it, and thrusts his hand into the sky.

Above us, the sound of the chopper pauses for a moment, starts again, and then chokes as the power dies. Sam shudders and falls to his knees, and this time I don't have it in me to catch him. I already have one body cradled in my arms, pressed against my cold chest—feet, fingers, and heart numb. In the sky, the engine roars again as the chopper starts to fall toward the slums. As soon as it's back under control, it banks and flies back over the Wall.

We stagger into a lean-to made of aluminum and plastic sheeting and see an old woman huddled in the corner. Well, old by slum standards—she's only thirty-five or so—but the haggard lines ingrained with dirt ruin her face. Her greasy hair is lank and wet, and her eyes are wild, flicking from side to side. She's flying on one of the street drugs. We ignore her. I set Abial down gently, using the dregs of my power to guide her, not wanting to drop the heavy weight.

The woman curses emphatically under her breath, seeing me floating a body to the floor, and bolts into the rain. I start after her for a split second, realize I wouldn't know what to do with her even if I caught up, and sag onto the uneven floor, instead.

The lean-to doesn't cut out the wet and wind, but it is a kind of shelter, even with the water streaming down the runnels in the "walls." For the moment, at least, we're safe. I lean over Abial, pressing my hand to her cheek, and communicating mentally. *Abial, hold on. Listen to me—we'll get you out of here—it's gonna be okay.* I try to inject my mind-to-mind speech with confidence, but can't hide the edge of panic, the feeling I'm breaking in half. I wish I'd paid more attention in the classes meant to help us separate emotion from sending. My thoughts are scattered and confused, splitting away from each other like light refracting through a prism, but I know Abial is getting a sense of everything filling me: fear, uncertainty, misery. Regret.

Abial shudders. *No.* She sends a wavering image of the chopper beam finding her as she stood, poised to jump, and then she heard the stuttering of Zap fire breaking the air as she went over. I curse and try to rip away her shirt to see the damage. As I do, I realize the flatpack Abial had been wearing is gone. All for nothing. It's gone. I count the noises Abial sent me. Eight Zap hits at close range. I know it's hopeless, and the knowledge must be painted starkly on my face. Abial's insides must be mush; not even a shockvest could dull that amount of energy.

Her hand clutches feebly, golden faded to an unnatural gray, and my lip trembles before I take her hand in my own. Skin to skin, our connection reignites. The pain drives a gasp from me. *Please don't.* I'm not even sure what I mean. Please don't hurt; please don't go; please don't die; please don't leave me. I can't look away from the pulverized mash of body armor mangling the torso of my oldest friend.

Abial opens her mind. *I'm sorry.* She shows me Kion, starting from the very first day they met. Abial, as a twelve-year-old slum kid, and Kion a dashing young operative. He saved her life, once, twice, and she was his from that moment, always. The following years she'd spent training, a closeness developed between them. Then the raid. Damon taken, months of watching Kion helping me train, looking after me, only paying attention to me, as though Abial no longer existed. Caught up by my intensity and purpose, our personalities fitting together. And all the while Abial *knowing* I was hiding something from her. But not that, never that. The only reason Abial took the test so early was to prove to Kion she wasn't a child anymore, and she was ready to fight. To fight for him, by his side. For a while, he'd looked at her again, seen her with those arresting, driven eyes, shadowed with all the pain she'd never shared.

Then I was ready to test. Abial shows the jealousy and hatred built up in her until she finally snapped, and I feel the roiling emotions as if they're my own, as Kion whispers, "She's amazing" over the ear comm units the defending operatives wore while they struggled to catch me in the Arena. The words had cut Abial to the core, laying a secret open that she was unwilling to face herself, and the pure pain and rage had boiled out of her, sculpted into an image she knew would make me feel her pain, her rage. There hadn't even been conscious thought to it, only a bitter outpouring of jealousy and hatred. Of love turned to dust.

*I didn't know. You never told me. You should have told me. He's my brother. Not my...* It's so stupid, so pointless, so wrong I can barely breathe with it. I bite my lip and send memories of me spending time with Abial, hanging out, talking, killing time and training together, playing with Damon—all the good memories I can muster. I wind my power into Abial's and help her block the burning pain of her ground-up organs, using techniques we learned together.

I let Abial see deep into my mind, farther than I ever have in all our years of closeness. I let her see my secrets. I let her see everything. Try to show her how wrong she was to suspect something romantic between me and Kion. How the feeling between us could never be that way. It's not even important, now, not really, but I don't want Abial to die thinking we were sneaking around behind her back. Feeling betrayed. It's as though I've been skinned alive, sharing the hurt Abial has carried. Tears streak my cheeks, following tracks left by the rain and dripping to the floor.

*Never?* Abial's hand tightens on mine.

*Never. I wasn't... I wasn't hiding feelings for him. Not for him.* For you. I don't need to send it, there's no point. Not now. If she didn't pick it out of my thoughts already, I don't need to lay it on her.

Abial relaxes a little, sighing, eyes fixed on what passes for a ceiling. Sam sits by Abial's head and combs her wet hair from her face, looking blank and shocked. We wait quietly, uselessly, and soon Abial's chest stutters and stills, her harsh breathing catching and dragging wet in her throat, then stopping. The silence beats in my ears until I sniff and drag my hand roughly across my face. "We have to go." I sound bleak, even to my own ears. I lost Abial. She's gone. I spent months hiding the way I felt from her and left a space for her to fill in the blanks with a betrayal.

I should have told her.

I watch with a strange detachment as my hands move of their own accord, business-like, closing Abial's eyes and removing her few personal effects. There's a picture of Kion and Abial playing Rizkball together, laughing. This I carefully slip into my chest pocket, and the rest of the odds and ends are put away without looking. I get to my feet, my joints creaking.

Sam grimaces and looks around. "Are we really leaving her...her body in that woman's house?" His voice breaks halfway through the sentence, and he has to clear his throat.

I shrug a shoulder and jerk my head at the gaping hole in the hut. "I can't carry her. I'm too weak. They'll find her wherever we leave her. They'll find us if we don't get gone. We don't have a choice. At least..." My voice cracks for a moment. "At least it's not raining on her in here."

I swallow, look at the body for a long second, and then duck out the gap serving as a door. Back into the night. Sam follows me hastily, clanging noisily against the entrance on his way out. I don't look back. I check my wrist unit robotically and lead us on in silence, my mind playing the evening over again and again. I catalog my injuries, keeping my mind veering away from a place threatening to collapse me. Chest: badly bruised, but nothing broken or cracked. Manageable. Face: cut, no problem. Knees: twisted, at least. Badly. I'm limping heavily, but have no power left to brace them, having spent the last dregs of it carrying Abial with us. Feet: sore, bruised, but nothing life-threatening for now. The dirt of the slums is deep in me, ingrained in my wounds and the creases of my skin. I'll need medicine, soon, to hold off the sickness.

I choke back a sob as I realize the place that hurts the most won't stop hurting, no matter what medicine I'm given. There's no cure for this. My heart is too big, too heavy for my chest; it's pulling me down and down into the mud, dragging me to the floor with the weight of the changes the night has wrought on me.

The journey is a meaningless blur. When the chopper throbs overhead, scanning for us, we duck into whatever shelter we can, startling groups of people hiding from the weather. I'd prefer to leave less of a trail; my bare feet will be leaving evidence of my passing, of my misery. I can only hope the rain will wash it away. But if these people are questioned psionically, it will be easy to follow us. I'm relying on the dwells having no love for the Watch, and knowing how to make themselves scarce.

Nobody interferes with us. Seeing the looks on our faces seems to be enough of a deterrent. Dawn is lightening the horizon to a paler shade of black when I finally check our position one last time and, furrowing my brows, rap lightly and rhythmically on the plastic sheet in front of us.

It's exactly the same as all the sheets around it—wet and grimy, haphazardly leaning against whatever has been scrounged up for a wall. I'm not entirely confident in my navigation, but thankfully, a returning knock is heard, and when I respond with the arranged answer, the sheet moves, screeching against the rough floor. A brown hand becomes visible, holding it back. "C'mon in, kids. The weather's terrible, ain't it?" The voice is so incongruously warm and cheerful in the desolation of the slums that my chest loosens, just a little, and I squat and shuffle through the gap.

Leaf promised we'd be safe here, for now. And so far, he's kept his word. I have no idea how to get home. Our mission is well and truly blown, Abial is dead and left behind, and I'm certain everyone in the Institute knows my face. The bag with Sam's all-important comm unit is lost somewhere, probably smashed when Abial was shot at the top of the Wall. All that information, gone. Worse, the tube will be crawling with Readers and Institute soldiers. To get back to Fourth City, we're going to have to go overland. And

I don't know how to make it work. Or if Sam could even attempt the journey. But I know I won't let myself die here, the way Abial did. I've already lost my oldest friend. I'm not willing to lose myself too. After all, if I get Sam home, the information he has might save us all.

# Part Seven

# Sam

WHAT'S IN THERE? Safety? It can't be! My throat tightens with tension as Serena squats and shuffles quickly into the gap, but I follow her lead, trusting she knows what she's doing. I can't imagine the Institute laying a trap for us out here in the muck, and so maybe, finally, we're safe...even for a moment. My eyes sting with the mere thought of it, but I refuse to relax too much, partially because I'm sure I'll fall over if I relax even one muscle.

It's a huge relief to be out of the rain and under some type of shelter, but the pervasive odor of sweat and rot coats the inside of my throat, as thick as paint. I struggle to swallow past the stench as a woman, hunched over in the low corridor, grins at us and then turns around. We make our way down a long but narrow hall in silence, the steep slope under my feet clearly taking us below ground. The walls of the tunnel are packed tight and there's no water on the ground, meaning it's probably in regular use.

Smugglers?

I've heard you can get all sorts of things you're not supposed to if you venture into the slums, and it stands to reason there has to be a way to transport stuff off the streets. So they must have a tunnel no one knows about. Does it mean an escape route for us? Will this passage get us out of the slums completely? I tamp down on the flair of hope. Smugglers aren't exactly reputed to be kind and welcoming, as far as I'm aware. I've seen the vids at school.

There's a huge black market for body parts, and I'm in possession of a nice clean set of lungs, and other cancer-free organs.

I scratch at my neck nervously, determined to put the thought of being dissected out of my mind, and struggle to keep up with the pace they're setting. There are lanterns every dozen feet, throwing circles of light out onto the firm brown walls and sandy ground. Every now and again we hit a T-junction and turn carefully, the space so tight as to be claustrophobic when in the corner. Everything looks the same, with passages spinning off in different directions, and I'm hopelessly lost after the first few turns, and fighting off a horrible vision of being abandoned here to wander until I finally pass out and die.

The scraping of our feet is the only sound breaking the heavy atmosphere, and the passage is stiflingly hot after being out in the cold rain. I'm grateful for the warmth at first, although it doesn't take long before my eyes are burning with sweat. I actually think I see steam rising off my sodden shirt, but I wouldn't be surprised if my mind was playing tricks on me.

After maybe ten minutes of rapid walking, we finally hit a flight of stairs and start up. My legs are burning by the time the woman opens a door to the outside world and motions us through.

I hesitate for a moment, not wanting to head back into the night. I just want to be safe, to stop running, and even though the soldiers could be right behind us—could have already found the entrance to the tunnel—being underground seems safer. I feel like an animal wanting to hide in a hole while the dogs bay at the entrance. But the woman cocks her head at me in question, so I clench my jaw and force a nod in thanks as I pass.

The door shuts behind us with an ominous and final-sounding clunk.

Someone melts out of the gloom so suddenly I start, knocking my back against the plastic sheeting with a boom that cuts the darkness, leaving me off balance and leaning against it awkwardly. The figure is wearing a hooded jacket, and although the light is poor, I make out high cheekbones and deep-set, sparkling eyes. I pick myself up, every movement slow and painful.

"Blimey, he's a smooth one, ain't he?" I can't even see the guy's mouth move in the shadows, but his voice is deep and thickly accented.

"Leaf!" Serena's voice is heavy with tears and exhaustion, and the person in front of us flicks his hood off, revealing thick black hair and a wicked grin edged with sadness. "Yep. I still got yer back. There's Readers all over; didn't want anyone else gettin' a look at you. Figured it was safer to use the tunnel to get you out here, where it's quiet. You're already too easy to follow, traipsin' around barefooted. Don't need you drawin' any more attention. We gotta go. Put some damn shoes on."

He waggles an object in his right hand, and I realize he's holding a pair of boots. How the hell did he know Serena lost her shoes? Who is this guy? He talks like a slum kid but knows Serena, and she obviously knows him. Is there history here? Is that what all the gibberish is about? Can he help us get out?

He steps forward, and Serena sniffs and gives him a quick hug, lifting his feet right off the floor. He gives a very unmanly squeak in surprise, looking deeply uncomfortable.

"Thanks," she breathes. There's a lot in the word. It's labored under her exhaustion, and the gratitude is palpable. She's obviously talking about more than a pair of boots. But Leaf only gives a nod in reply.

I squirm awkwardly under the weight of the nonconversation, wanting to get going, and my back actually itches as we wait for Serena to yank the shoes on. We're exposed, and the rain is easing off. The only reason I'm still alive is the rain covered my tracks, washing my psionic residue away and keeping people off the street so I wasn't reported at every turn. Though I'm starting to believe I'll never be dry again, cold and damp to the bone, I'm scared to see the rain fading. I tilt my head back to get a drink, at least. Fluids might keep me going for a little longer.

Leaf laughs softly at me, but there's no cruelty in it, and I want to ask who he is, what he's doing here. I want to know if he's armed, if he's dangerous, and most of all, if he has a place for us to rest, but before I gather the nerve, Serena has the shoes on, and Leaf is moving forward at a fast pace. Serena and I straggle after him, both of us exhausted and clumsy.

He flaps a hand at us when we reach the end of the alley—obviously a sign to wait—and I hear the low murmur of conversation when I concentrate. There must be a group of people walking on the street ahead. I guess we're staying here until they pass.

While we're hiding in the shadow of an overhang, he looks back at Serena, his lean face taking on a serious cast, and places his hand, palm flat, over the center of his chest.

"I carry her with me." The whispered words have the weight of ritual—something serious I don't understand sucking the air out of the alley.

She almost chokes on the reply. "And I thank you for your aid."

Abial. They're talking about Abial. How does he know about her? The same way he knew Serena needed shoes, I guess. He must have had people watching us. I shiver at the idea of people following us while we've been running, at our wits' end and so alone. Why didn't they help us, if they knew where we were and what was happening? Is she sure she can trust this guy?

A yell from the alley ahead makes me jump, but Leaf doesn't look worried, and we continue to wait awkwardly. I want to repeat the words he's said, though I don't feel as if I should...like I'd be intruding on a private moment. After a small pause, though, I put my dripping hand over my soaking heart as well. Abial saved me just as much as Serena did, even if she wasn't the one talking me down in the room. She was her partner. They were in it together; she risked her life against the soldiers while Serena came into my hiding place. And there's no way we would have gotten over the Wall without her. I'd be dead without her, many times over.

Leaf's eyes flick toward me, and he nods in a short jerk of approval. "Alrighty, like the lady said, I'm Leaf. Let's move. We need you out of sight by dawn, or you're dead."

He's walking before he's finished his sentence, shrugging a bag off his shoulder and fishing out two packs of protein gel—powershots—then thrusting one at me. I grab it eagerly, ripping it open, almost walking into a wall as I upend it, welcoming the taste of chemical energy that usually makes me gag. You can kill yourself running only on these, but they'll keep you on your feet long past what's naturally possible, and it's been another long time since I've eaten anything. Energy surges in my blood, my heart pounds, and my lungs swell easily in my chest.

I look up, and Serena has spots of color in her cheeks that must match my own hot face. She's eaten hers, as well, and has renewed energy, tapping on her wrist unit until the screen glows dully green. With the boost, we manage to speed up, almost jogging through the drizzle and mud.

"If you can get us to the desert, we'll need a sheet to make a still to get water. Food would be great, but I can catch lizards, which is better than carrying extra weight."

I gulp. The desert. I guess I sort of knew we only had one option. You can't hide from mind readers in the City, not really. So the only way we're going to stay alive is distance, and getting on the Tube for the journey isn't an option. But the desert? It will take us days of walking to get to another City, or are we planning to hide out in the dunes until someone picks us up?

No, that's not possible, because the Institute would just track us to wherever we were. Leaf said we had to get out of sight by dawn; I suppose so no one from the slums catches a glimpse and gives away our location, meaning the Readers will have to follow in our footsteps, looking for signs of our passing. And they'll be slower than if they head straight for us. Still, we won't be able to rest until we're out of sight, and even then, I'd bet they'll have vehicles after us.

How can we get away from armored cars on foot? We won't stand a chance! We can't hide, and we don't have a shot in hell of getting far enough away if we're trying to outrun vehicles. I don't understand what the plan can possibly be. I want to ask, but they're still talking as if I'm not even here.

"No time. I have a map for you, where you can cut cacti for water, but other than that, you've got these bottles." He passes them over. "I hope you can climb, 'cause we're taking the high road."

I want to gulp, but I suppress it and try to look confident. I'm juddering with pent-up energy from the powershot, so maybe that'll give me what I need to follow them. I know for a fact they'll have no option but to leave me if I can't, so there's no choice, really. "No problem."

He gives another nod, then slides noiselessly into the darkness. Somewhere behind us, an engine roars faintly, and Serena and I exchange fearful glances, then break into a run.

We travel another block in ragged silence until Leaf suddenly ghosts up a wall with such easy steps it looks as though he's flying. Serena gestures for me to follow, but my hands are shaking as I step forward, looking up at the wall. I made it up the rope in gym class, I remind myself as I run my hands over the ragged, ancient brickwork, hunting for handholds before I start to climb.

It's tough going, the rough surface skinning my hands until my grip is slicked with blood. My soles slip frequently, but somehow I never actually fall and finally scramble up onto the flat surface of the roof. I'm sure Serena must have wedged lumps of power under my feet on the shakier steps, but when she slides onto the dilapidated roof moments after me, she doesn't say a word.

My heart pounds while we traverse roof after roof as fast as we can, my breathing harsh and loud. Our only footholds are sliding lumps of rubble and concrete, bolstered in places by carefully bent pitons of iron, and every time I jump from one to the next my heart skips a beat, expecting this to be the one that dumps me through to the ground far below.

The only noises are our scrabbling footsteps and the light, now-incessant patter of rain, the going slow and fraught with hazards. I'm sweating freely from a mixture of terror and exertion, my armpits chafed and feet sore by the time the edge of the slums comes into sight. When we arrive, I peer over the side, eyes wide.

There's no way I can descend the smooth sheet of metal to the ground below. We're at least two stories up, everything rickety and unstable, and I doubt Serena has the strength to catch me the way she did when I flew down the Wall. But Leaf rolls his eyes at me and fishes around on the edge of the roof, looking for something. Then he swings his leg over, grins, and starts to descend. Before I've figured out what he's using, he's out of sight, using an invisible climbing route.

Gathering my nerve, I risk a glance back over the path we've traveled. To my horror, I see torches flashing only a few streets behind us, and another surge of fear and adrenaline races through me. The soldiers—they've found us. Knowing now I always go in the middle, I jump toward the edge. Looking down makes my stomach churn, but I make out huge nails hammered into the sheet of metal and bent sideways to form impossibly small steps.

There's no time for my panic, so I clench my jaw and sit. Then I have to roll onto my stomach and grope for the first nail. Serena hovers above me impatiently, but clearly ready to grab my hand if I need her. Reassured, I blindly move my foot from side to side until it hits what I'm looking for. The next one is easier, and I follow Leaf onto the treacherous "ladder," terror moving my feet for me. The last foothold is more of a toehold, and as I shift my weight, my foot cramps. Unable to support myself with the two fingers I have hooked through one of the handholds, I teeter away from the building, arms pinwheeling.

I'm falling, already tensing for the impact, when fingertips dig violently into my armpits and my back smacks against Leaf's chest. He's caught me and holds on until I find my feet, which are on a shifting pile of sand and small rocks. The ground—I've reached the ground. Serena drops lightly next to me, not even having bothered to climb. She's full of nervous energy, hands twitching at nothing as she questions me.

"You okay?"

I nod, and Leaf looks up, dusting himself off.

"Yeah. They're right behind us, though. I'll see if I can stall 'em. You better run. Good luck!" Then he spins and sprints down a nearby path, jinking around a corner before either of us can say anything else.

Serena and I look at each other, stricken. We're both barely still on our feet, and I thought for sure he'd stay with us. How's he going to slow them down? What can one guy do against so many?

Without another glance after him, though, Serena starts jogging, and I scramble after her, barely catching her hissed sentence. "He's a bit of a weirdo, but a good bloke. Reliable." The way she says it tells me he's come through for her before, and I nod.

"Can he stall them, really? The desert..." I trail off, breathing raggedly. She knows. People live in the townships, scraping by with nothing because anything is better than the wasteland dividing the Cities. Even the desert tribes would call it idiotic to head out with no water or equipment. The sun is a brutal killer in the slums, where there's shade, but there's nowhere to shelter from it in the dunes.

And we have to get across. Alone. Out of sight before dawn, and far enough away so the soldiers can't track us and drag us back to the Institute to rot. Or kill us. I still don't know if we can do it, but I don't have any choice. So I gulp, settle my shoulders, and jog after Serena into the desert.

MY BOOTS SLIDE on the sandy grit, which gets thicker and thicker as we enter the desert proper until it's all that's under my feet. The last of the ruined buildings falls behind us, and eventually, they're nothing but shadows hunching on the horizon when I glance back. My calf muscles ache within moments, and when I change my gait to compensate, the burn in my thighs builds up. It's going to be a long journey. There's a lot that could kill us out here—the heat, exhaustion, sunstroke—not to mention the dozens of poisonous species that thrive in the wastes, and the traders who travel from City to City. Oh yeah, and we've only a little water, and barely any food.

And the Institute and Watch are right on our heels. They might not have pinned our trail inside the slums yet, but it's only a matter of time.

I shake off the thought with vicious determination and force myself forward, the sand sucking at my feet as we head into the velvet night. Serena sets the pace, and I know we could go faster, but we wouldn't last long. Not before we burned out completely. We're both too tired.

The rain fades out after a few miles, and the farther we get from the City, the more stars pop into sight in the black vista above us. We'll be easier to spot now, and Serena increases our speed a little, so I assume it's freaking her out as much as it is me. Huge dunes force us to travel diagonally, throwing us off our path and meaning we gain little ground. Then the wind picks up, tugging at our clothing and adding to the general misery of the trek. My feet drag with every step, reminding me people who are far better prepared than us die in the desert—exhausted, miserable, and totally unready for what's ahead.

We've been walking for long enough I can't even remember what it's like to walk without my legs screaming, and then something changes. I'm following her footsteps, trying to pay attention, my head fuzzy with exhaustion and thirst, when she cocks her head. It looks as though she's listening, so I close my eyes and cast out my power, shocked at how weak it is; the trek and lack of sleep and food have almost exhausted my reserves.

I can't feel anything near us with my power, but perhaps my range is totally shot. What's out there? What does she hear?

Then I hear it too. A throbbing in the air, low and unrelenting. An engine. I look wildly in a circle, searching for a chopper, but can't pick out anything in the black sky. Wait, there, a shadow? Did a chopper pass in front of a star?

Serena grabs my arm, startling me, and pulls me backward down a slope, so quickly I almost fall on my ass. I'm hit in the back of the legs on the way, whatever it is tearing holes in the fabric of my trousers with sharp claws, and I stumble. My lightning reaction is the only thing stopping me from toppling right over. Instead, I twist my body around, trying to figure out what's happened.

A cactus—huge, towering up into the sky, easily twice my height. I hit one of its lower arms with my calves, which are wet and sticky—with blood or cactus juice, I can't tell. It stings, either way. Is it poisonous? My legs burn, but I can't tell if it's only cuts...or worse working its way into my bloodstream. If it is poison, what will happen? Will I be able to keep going, or will I pass out, forcing Serena to leave me behind?

She drags me past the cactus, not caring about my injury, and I'm about to voice a complaint when I remember, abruptly, we were running away from a sound when I fell. My brain isn't working properly, and that's dangerous. How could I have forgotten we heard an engine only moments ago? Now I'm concentrating again, I pick the noise out—a recursive whine rather than the beating of rotors.

Land, not sky. ATVs, probably. I close my eyes to concentrate and reach out, looking for their connections. If I can cut their power, we might gain a few precious seconds and get deeper into the paltry protection offered by the cacti. As exhausted as we are, we don't stand a chance in a fair fight, let alone against a dozen soldiers or so, all armed. Looking for their wiring takes me a few stumbling footsteps, and I have to trust Serena to guide me around the huge plants by which we're surrounded.

I count two engines closing on the top of the dune we're running down, but I'm too fried to cut their power, my gift skittering and squirming away from me. So we sprint instead, as quietly as we can, ducking through the towering plants snatching at us with their sharp needles. The engine noise is getting louder and louder, headlights flashing and catching brief snapshots of the needles and limbs we're racing through. My chest is tight, as if I'm about to have a heart attack, and my legs wobble beneath me, threatening to give out.

Then Serena thumps into something and trips, sprawling facedown in the gritty sand, barely missing the nearest spiky hazard. I skid to a halt and grab her arm to help her up, but she wriggles around and freezes, eyes fixed on a hump on the shadowy ground.

Above us, the engine noise stops and a voice calls, "You're under arrest. Come out with your hands clasped on top of your heads."

An ominous buzzing is picking up, reverberating uncomfortably through my jawbone. What kind of weapon do they have that could make a noise like that?

Serena's hand clasps around my wrist hard enough to make me wince, and she hisses, "You have to run. I'll hold them off. You have to get to ARC."

I shake my head. "Don't be an idiot. Look, they don't know we're here; we can still sneak away. They're just guessing." I think.

"I can't move."

"Are you hurt? Throw your arm over my shoulder, I'll help you. If we slide down here, we can make our way through this valley." I'm desperate, now; if she can't go on, we're done. I crouch down in the darkness and tug at her arm weakly. The buzzing is getting louder, though, and suddenly her body jerks slightly, tensing as though in an electric current. She grits her teeth.

"Even if they didn't have Readers, who probably already know we're in the area, I have my foot in the entrance to a sand wasp nest. My boot's stuck. And they're stinging me through the material. The poison's already in my bloodstream, so I'm as good as dead. If I move my foot, they'll kill you too."

She delivers the news in such a matter-of-fact tone I don't process it for a moment. Right then, up on the top of the dune, light flares. The soldiers have stuck a glow beacon in the ground, and it illuminates the world for twenty paces. They'll keep planting new ones, keeping themselves out of the immediate light circle so we can't shoot them, and soon the area will be lit up like a stadium.

Her foot is stuck. And if she breaks the nest to get out, the sand wasps will sting us to death in moments. I've only ever seen someone stung by sand wasps once before, on a vid. They didn't even look like a person by the time the wasps were finished. Their insides were liquefied by the overdose of poison, and the wasps would have crawled into the carcass and laid their eggs if it'd been left there.

I shiver. I'd prefer a quick death by Zapfire, I reckon.

For about half a second I consider doing as she says—leaving her with the soldiers and the wasps. Maybe she'd manage to shoot everyone before she succumbed to the poison—passed out and choked to death, her airway closed up, as she was stung more and more, the poison permeating every milliliter of blood. But I shake the thought off. Not a chance. I wouldn't even be here if she hadn't gotten me out of the City, and I'm not leaving her.

Suddenly, I hear a muffled noise maybe thirty feet away from us. A soldier losing footing, I guess. And there are others with him, I'm sure; they'll be on us in a moment. We're running out of time. Serena gasps in pain, her fist clenching around my wrist so tightly I think it's going to break before she lets go. Another sting, I guess.

How many times can a person get stung before they die? I think it depends on height and weight. And she's small. She won't have long.

"Actually, if I unlace your boot, can you use your power to keep the wasps trapped under it?" It might buy us a second or two. It would be better if she could create a shield now, for her foot, but obviously she'd be doing it already if she was able to. She's stronger than any Psi I've heard of in my research on the Institute over the past few days, but that doesn't mean she's invincible.

She grimaces again and nods. Then another flare of light bursts up above us, illuminating the area to within ten paces of where we're lying. One more and they'll have us lit up like hunted animals. We have to move. Now.

I reach for her leg, feeling my way over her calf to her boot.

"Oh, sure, cop a feel." Her murmured joke is half-hearted at best, but it steadies my trembling fingers, and I try not to think about the incredibly poisonous insects inches from my skin. The knot in her laces is tight when I find it, worn by walking and clotted with dust. It takes too long to untie, and I'm about to shrug off my pack to get a knife when light explodes around us.

I freeze, throwing my hands up, stomach heaving in anticipation of the energy blast. Then I realize the light isn't shining in my eyes. I open them slowly, petrified, expecting to see soldiers all around me, and almost throw up in relief when I see the soldiers have actually gone slightly downhill of us. The desert to my left is in sharp relief, the newest light circle only inches from the edge of my boot. They've very nearly found us.

But not yet. Not quite.

I slowly creep my foot inward and then return my attention to the knot, tearing at it frantically. A sharp pain bursts below my knuckle, and I bite my tongue. My first sting. It's like holding my hand over an open flame. Serena has every muscle tensed, knotted and spasming. If this is what she's going through, she must be in agony. And I don't think she has very long left until the toxin starts to get to her. Right as I'm about to give up, the lace gives, and I ease the tongue of her boot loose with shaking hands.

"Ready?" My whisper is so quiet it's nigh inaudible, but she taps her fingers against my hip, giving me permission.

I whip her foot out, and she flicks her hand forward, just in time. Two dark spots are worming over the lip of the boot, but freeze in place, then retreat as she pushes at them with her power. She has them trapped, for the moment.

"I can't walk."

I've already realized this—obvious as soon as her foot was free. It must be twice the size it should be, flesh ballooning and dark.

A shout breaks the darkness, making us both jump, and Serena slides her hand into mine. "You can still go—head up, through the dark. I'll slow them down." She sounds as if she's tired enough she'd prefer it, as though she's already decided to die here in the dark.

I squeeze her hand gently and don't even bother to reply. She should know I'm not going to leave her. At least she's not being stung anymore with her power holding the wasps off. Though it will only last until she passes out. I can't carry her, though—I can barely carry myself—so we're stuck.

The soldiers are right there. I hope they shoot us on sight.

The seconds scrape past, every sound in the dark ocean of desert sending another wave of adrenaline pounding through me, only to recede when nobody shoots. They're closing in, making a C shape around us, right into the valley below, and I think they must have a general read on our location and are working their way in toward us. We don't have long.

The light crawls closer and closer, but all we can do is wait. Serena lies on the ground, pale and shaking, a thin layer of her power the only thing between us and an ugly death. When I think about it, I realize there's an ugly death waiting for us on both sides.

Then my heart stutters as I have what is almost certainly a terrible idea. It might not work. But we don't have anything left to lose.

I bend down and put my lips as close to her ear as possible. "I have an idea. I'm going to see where the soldiers are. Wait here."

Even in her clammy, poisoned state, she's fully able to give me the "where do you think I'm gonna go, idiot" look. I grin shakily and turn to crawl through the darkness. My plan won't work if the soldiers aren't kind of close together. I need to know where they are, and I need to do it quickly. My hand is already numb from the single sting I received, and the soldiers will have us dead to rights in a few minutes.

Sand scratches at me, desiccated cactus needles skewering my stomach and thighs as I move, copying the military knees-and-elbows wriggle I've seen in war movies. But it's incredibly hard, so I give up, flopping onto my belly and worming forward as best I can. My stung hand is swollen, sausage fingers difficult to move or put pressure on, but I try to ignore the radiating pain. Stopping behind a large barrel cactus, I peer into the gloom.

Where are they? Where are the men trying to kill, or worse—capture—us?

I see the shapes moving as they search the cactus field, staying out of the light circles, and from my vantage point above them I count seven shadowy figures. But seven doesn't make sense; I felt two vehicles, so surely there would be...eight soldiers. I scan the shadowy land again and still see only seven.

Someone is missing.

Nothing I can do about it now. This will either work, or it won't. It's the only card I have left in my shitty, shitty deck. The seven of them are moving in sync, pacing forward and holding out their hands, clearly scanning the area. They're only meters away, but down a sharp drop, at the base of the slope. I knew they were downhill from me, but this is better than I'd hoped. A steep section is blocking the light from flowing up onto this side, so they'll never see what's coming for them.

After a few minutes, they turn and head back toward one another, regrouping. And for a moment, they're all together. It's now or never.

I crouch run back to Serena, no time to pick my way carefully now. I have to do this while they're standing in one place. She's lying where I left her, balled up in the fetal position, her foot still swollen, and now her face as well. She looks up at me from puffy, red eyes and tries to grin, but fat lips make it into an ugly rictus.

I try to smile reassuringly at her, although my heart is in my throat. If this works, we might actually make it out alive, but it's more likely I'm about to get stung to death. Still, thinking about it won't change anything, and I do it before I can think any more about it.

I grab the sand wasp nest in my left hand—a huge ball of clotted sand and dirt.

The buzzing from inside rises to a crescendo, the boot the only thing blocking the entrance. But not for long. I sprint back through the night, and have taken only five paces when the pain starts—starbursts in my fingers, my palm, the backs of my hand as the power holding the wasps disintegrates, and they start escaping. I almost drop the nest, but I can't—I can't yet.

I reach the edge of the drop and almost plunge right over as the ground pulls away from my feet. Somehow, I manage to hold on to my only weapon and my balance. The pain is incredible, and I choke as I throw the ball of wasps down the hill. It hits the ground once, then twice, and the soldiers turn and sprint toward the noise. They must think it's us—they've found us.

Before they take three steps, though, the nest bursts open in a cloud of death, which swarms outward in a vicious, pitch-black mass. It descends on the soldiers immediately, drawn toward their scent, and far enough away from me and Serena, as I hoped, we have escaped the notice of the insects. For now. When they've finished with the soldiers, they'll come after us. But that's a problem for future Sam.

In the meantime, the screams are horrible, and my own hand is swelling almost beyond recognition, fat and puffy, a rubber glove blown to bursting point. The skin will split open soon, unable to take the strain. I have to hurry.

I stagger back to my fallen companion and prod her in the side. "Up, come on. Up." The words come out in globs, dripping from a tongue twice its normal size. I'm reacting to the toxin quickly. Faster than I expected.

Serena makes a groaning noise, and retches, so I leave her and lurch through the darkness, struggling up the hill.

Suddenly a man bursts out of the murky gloom, almost bowling me over. He's past me before I realize it's the last soldier. He must have been waiting with the vehicles, maybe communicating with their base. He's heard his friends, and no wonder. I still hear them groaning and crying. Choking on wet noises, meat being hit with a tenderizing hammer.

Then an ATV is in front of me, wonderfully solid, and right where I hoped to find it. My other hand is starting to swell in response to the venom, and I fumble with the door handle, my fat, sweaty fingers sliding uselessly across the metal. I don't have time for this, I think, panicked. I'm almost crying, my throat closing as I struggle.

And then finally the door clicks open. I half fall through the yawning gap, fumbling with the canvas netting strapped to the sides of the seating area. I grasp under the seats, searching...searching...

Then I find it. A box, a plastic box. I haul it out, heart pounding. If I'm this sick, this quickly, Serena might already be dead. The box is orange, marked with a green cross—first aid. Struggling for air, breathing through a straw made of my own flesh, it takes forever to unclasp the fiddly plastic catches and yank open the case. I throw medical supplies wildly out of my way, vision swimming and chest being squeezed by a giant fist. Then my bloated fingers find a tube encased in packaging. I haul it out, peering at it desperately. But I can't make out the writing.

Epi— Epine— It has to be epinephrine, and if it's not, I'm dead anyway. I make a hash of the packing, tearing it open with my teeth, and uncapping it the same way. I'm falling back out of the vehicle even as I drive the needle into the meat of my thigh.

I stop breathing.

The world goes black.

My blood has been replaced with electricity, surging through me, faster than blood should ever go. I'm aware of every inch of my skin, the grains of sand caught in my belt, the prickle of hair on my calves. It's terrifying, and then the pressure on my chest releases, a snapping band. Cold air surges into my chest in a donkey-kick explosion, and I cough, choking on my own breath. For a few moments, I lie there, weak and wrung out, totally useless. And then, aching and shivering, I force myself up. Serena.

I stumble to the other vehicle, and it's easier. The fluid swelling my body is already receding, run over by modern medicine. I find the second needle and shamble into the dark, back to where I left my friend. She's curled on her side when I arrive, totally still. The needle already out of its packing, I drop to my knees—which complain viciously as I land—praying I'm not too late. Ignoring the pain, I jab the needle into the flesh of her buttock, since it's closest, and then collapse, jerking like a fish on the line.

The world fractures into pain and darkness.

HER MOAN ROUSES me from my stupor, and I cough as I wake up fully. The soft light of dawn is streaking the sky, and I see a lot more of what's around me. The cacti are silhouetted against the lightening sky, but there are no soldiers or sand wasps—thank Google—in sight. Pulling myself up onto one elbow, I poke at her back with still-clumsy fingers and she groans, reassuring me. I close my eyes in relief. She's alive. We're both alive.

But dawn is here, and we're out of time. The soldiers we killed will be missed, and soon. I choke as I roll into a sitting position, my whole body weak and screaming.

"Serena. Serena." I sound like a rusty lawnmower, but she stirs with a grunt.

Her face is speckled with broken veins and still puffed out and soft-looking. I imagine I look, if anything, worse. I took more stings than her, I think. But I got the medicine sooner and managed to save us both. The pride and relief fuels me enough to crawl to my knees, and then, painfully, to my feet.

Serena manages to get up a moment later, and we stagger up the hill, arms over each other's shoulders, hauling our trashed bodies to the ATV. It takes us a few minutes to find water in the panels of the door, and I rummage through the scattered first aid kit to find painkillers and a powershot. It's time we have to take—I can barely see through blurry eyes, and my whole body is screaming at me to collapse, to stop struggling and sleep. But I'm horribly aware of the light in the sky as I force myself to clamber into the passenger seat. We'll be easily spotted in daylight, and though we have a vehicle now, it will be difficult to stay ahead of the soldiers I know are coming after us.

I'm waiting for Serena to get into the driver's seat and take charge, but she scowls as she looks at me, her face mushy and pale, eyes bloodshot and sore. "I'm a shitty driver."

She's clearly serious, and an unexpected laugh makes me cough again, causing me to hack up vile green fluid. I struggle to hawk it out of the open window, into the sand. But the medicine we took is kicking in, and I nod, the chemical energy fizzing in my blood. Painkillers plus powershots; I'm high as a kite and on death's door, but what's a few hours' drive over impossible terrain compared to what we've already been through?

I crawl into the driver's seat and pull the seat belt on with difficulty, feeling a hundred years old. "You can navigate."

She scrapes her dirty hair off her forehead and shoves our packs awkwardly into the back seat. "Deal." The comm is in her hand before I've found first gear.

I glance at the dash, then look again, shocked. The ATV's equipped with fancy radar, and there are already flashing green blobs on it, coming up behind us. Quickly. Soldiers, and if they're on our screen, we're on theirs too. How long before they figure out we killed the people who are supposed to be in this vehicle? They might already know.

We have to get out of here.

I floor the accelerator, and the machine careens down the hill, narrowly avoiding cactus after cactus, and bouncing over unseen gullies. The engine screams at me when I crunch the gears, and I correct myself hurriedly, thankful for all the time I've "wasted" playing driving games. But I probably shouldn't tell Serena I've only been behind the wheel a half dozen times before. The sand kicks up behind our vehicle, wind whipping it into mini tornados, and I hope it hides our tire tracks.

For the first time, I believe we have a fighting chance of making it to her City—to salvation. And as I listen to her talking into the comm, I realize she's asking for someone to meet us. A welcoming committee to spirit us away. To somewhere with beds. I actually glaze over for a moment, trying to remember what it's like to relax, and am jerked back to reality with a bump as the ATV starts sliding down the side of a huge dune. Frowning in concentration, I fumble with the dash and smile when I find what I'm looking for.

Music roars out of the speakers when I press Play, and Serena dives forward to lower the volume. But I nod my head to the beat as I focus on the uneven terrain, hoping the music will help me stay alert. It's an eight-hour drive. All I have to do is stay awake and not crash. After what I've been through, that sounds like a piece of cake.

I push the accelerator down as far as it can go and grin as the huge wheels tear into the desert sand. According to the screen, we have a few miles on the soldiers coming after us. And we aren't searching for anyone.

Which means, with luck, we might just make it.

# Acknowledgements

I always read the acknowledgements at the backs of books I've loved, so first of all, thanks to you, reader, for making it this far and wanting to hang on to this book for a little longer. Writing a book is a solitary act that requires (at least for me) immense amounts of support from the people around me. Publishing a book requires even more. I have a large list of people to thank, and each and every one of them deserves more than a brief line in the back here, but that's what you get!

First off, thanks to my team at NineStar Press who coparented this book with me until it was ready to leave home. Rae, BJ and my amazing copy editors, thank you for your time, hand-holding and support. Next, Marie, my partner and cheerleader, teammate, and best friend. Couldn't have done it without you, love, and I mean that quite literally because of the many times you sternly told me to go and write when I was procrastinating, as well as all the times you trouble-shot with me and figured out my plot holes. Alix, my external hard drive, amazing friend, and kick-ass writer pal: thank you for knowing the answers to my weirdly specific questions, and for not getting mad when I text you first thing in the morning.

My parents, who never once told me to get a real job while I was trying the writing thing full time, but gave me their love and support instead. My sister, Alex, for all the encouragement and medical advice (super handy to know a doctor when you're writing a book, as it turns out), and brother in law, Dave, for general excellence. I'm so lucky to have you all on my team! The incredible Mary Fan (who is a wildly talented author you should check out) has been a bastion of support and care and help for me right from when I took my first wobbly steps into the publishing industry. My cheerleading team; Sinead, Lori, Meryl, Max, Mish, Alice, Lianna, Dylan, Jessie, thanks for every time you told me 'you can do this!'

Team bookfriends, Ali, Leah, Danny and Jeremy, you've kept me going when things got tough. My sibs-in-law, Eva and Kyle, for being excited and supportive even when things kept stalling, thanks for everything along this journey. Team Morgan-Boalch, Team Tann, Team MacMillan, I love you a lot! I'd also be remiss if I didn't mention Sam MacNeil, who reignited my passion at a time when I was struggling; their enthusiasm for my series really helped me get 'er done. Thanks also to Ken, my resident military expert who helped me with my weaponry.

And last but not least, everyone who wanted more of my writing and took the time to let me know via my website, reviewing, or social media. You have no idea how much every message and review means to me.

# About the Author

Tash is a Computer Science and English teacher in Canada, although they were born and raised in the hilly sheepland of Wales (and have lived in South Korea and Chile before settling down in Vancouver). Tash identifies as trans and queer and uses the neutral pronoun 'they.' As an English teacher they are fully equipped to defend that grammar!

They have a degree in computer science so their nerd chat makes sense, and a couple of black belts in karate, which are very helpful when it comes to writing fight scenes.

Their novel writing endeavors began at the age of eight, although they will admit their first attempt was derivative, at best. Since then, Tash has spent time falling in streams, out of trees, juggling, dreaming about zombies, dancing, painting, learning, and then teaching karate, running away with the circus, and of course, writing.

They write fast-paced, plot-centric action adventure with diverse casts. They write the books they wanted to read as a queer kid and young adult (and still do!)

Email: tash.mcadam@gmail.com

Facebook: www.facebook.com/tashmcadam

Twitter: @tashmcadam

Website: www.tashmcadam.com

# Also Available from NineStar Press

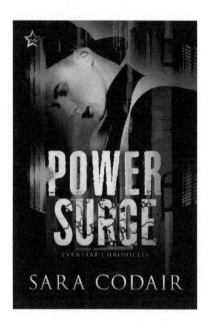

# Connect with NineStar Press

Website: NineStarPress.com

Facebook: NineStarPress

Facebook Reader Group: NineStarNiche

Twitter: @ninestarpress

Tumblr: NineStarPress